Ship of Fools

From the Tales of Dan Coast

By: Rodney Riesel

Published by Island Holiday Publishing

East Greenbush, NY

ISBN: 978-0-9894877-4-0

First Edition

Special thanks to:

Pamela Guerriere

Kevin Cook

Cover Design by:

Connie Fitsik

To learn about my other books friend me at

https://www.facebook.com/rodneyriesel

For Brenda,
Kayleigh, Ethan
& Peyton

KEY LARGO

ISLAMORADA

MARATHON

BIG PINE KEY &
THE LOWER KEYS

KEY WEST

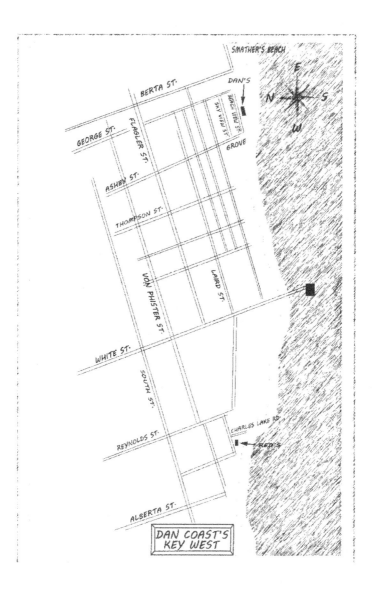

DAN COAST'S
KEY WEST

Chapter One

Dan Coast sat in a dark brown leather chair with wooden arms and wooden legs. His fingers were laced behind his head, his legs were crossed and stretched out in front of him, and his feet rested on a walnut desk that glistened from several coats of hand-applied gloss polyurethane. He stared at the diploma that hung on the wall behind the desk, just as he had done five days a week for the last six weeks from eleven o'clock in the morning until noon.

THE AMERICAN BOARD OF PSYCHIATRY AND NEUROLOGY, INCORPORATED 1934, MEMBER OF THE AMERICAN BOARD OF BLAH, BLAH, BLAH, BLAH. Dan had read it some twenty odd times over the past few weeks and he still wasn't impressed. As far as he was concerned it may as well have said Florida State Bartending School.

The door knob jiggled, there was a pause, and then it jiggled again.

"Lift up when you turn!" Dan hollered.

The door knob turned and the door opened. "Thank you," said the man in the gray pin-striped suit, as he entered and closed the door behind him. The man appeared to Dan to be in his late forties. He was a little taller than Dan and a bit thinner with brown, shaggy, shoulder-length hair that didn't quite go with the suit.

Dan marveled at the man's Thomas Magnum-like mustache. *Wish I had the balls to grow one of those*, he thought. He watched as the man searched the desk for something.

Not finding what he was after, he suddenly turned to Dan. "Dan Coast?" he asked.

"Nope," Dan replied.

He lowered his brow. "You're not Dan Coast?"

Dan slowly shook his head back and forth. "Nope."

"Huh. I must have my times confused. Sorry about that." The man walked back to the door and went out. This time he lifted the handle as he turned.

Dan sat quietly for a few moments and looked around the dark, paneled room at the many shelves filled with stodgy medical books and journals. A walnut-colored ceiling fan spun lazily above his head.

The door opened again and Shaggy walked back into the room. He was carrying a file folder this time.

"Very funny, Mr. Coast," he said. But he was not laughing, he wasn't even smiling.

"Thank you. I've often been praised for my comedic talent." Dan flashed an ear to ear smile that seemed to annoy the man even more.

"Yes, I've read your file, Mr. Coast. You're a real cut-up."

"You can just call me Dan."

"And you can just call me Dr. Richards. I'll be taking over for Dr. Morris from this point on," he said as he scanned the papers the folder contained.

"Where *is* Barbara?" Dan asked.

"*Dr. Morris* no longer works here."

"Yeah," Dan said, nodding in agreement. "It happens all the time." He turned his head and stared out the window at the blue sky.

Dr. Richards peered over the folder. "What happens all the time, Mr. Coast?"

"Girls like that make a killin' stripping to put themselves through college and then when they finish school and get out into the real world they see the hours are longer, the job is tougher, the pay is a lot less, and eventually they return to their old habits," Dan replied matter-of-factly.

Dr. Richards face tightened. "Barbara— I mean Dr. Morris —was not, nor has she ever been, an exotic dancer. She was a much-respected member of our staff here. She is simply leaving because she has found a better position at another place of employment."

Ha, better position, Dan thought. "Huh. She looked like a porn star," Dan responded, cupping his own giant imaginary breasts. "*You* know what I mean."

"Mr. Coast, why don't we drop this discussion and start a new one about you."

"Okay, Doc, sounds good." Dan pointed at the couch against the wall. "Would you like me on the couch or here in the chair?"

"Wherever you're most comfortable, Mr. Coast. Were you on the couch with Dr. Morris?"

"No, Sigmund," Dan sighed. "I think she wanted to keep ours a more professional relationship. But don't think I didn't try."

"I see you don't like to call people by the names they would prefer you to," Dr. Richards said.

"I don't follow."

"Well, for example, you refer to Dr. Morris by her first name, and you just referred to me as Sigmund, a reference to a well-known psychotherapist, instead of calling me Dr. Richards as I requested."

"Oh, no, Doc, you got it all wrong. It's that stupid hairdo of yours. Looks like a tangled pile of seaweed. You remind me of Sigmund the Sea Monster. You know, from the old Saturday morning kids show, Sigmund and the Sea Monsters, with that Johnny Whitaker kid from Family Affair. So I'll call you Sigmund, if you don't mind."

"I do mind."

"Well, would you prefer I referred to you as Blurp or Slurp?" Dan analyzed the doctor's glazed expression and added, "They were Sigmund's brothers."

Dr. Richards slowly closed the file folder, leaned back against the desk, and stared at Dan for a few dumbfounded moments as he rubbed his mustache with his thumb and index finger. Dan stared back, still wishing he, too, had a mustache of the doctor's caliber.

"You know, Mr. Coast, according to Dr. Morris' notes, you haven't really shown any progress during your stay with us. But I'm going to make sure we change that."

"Well, Sigmund, ya better make it quick because I only got one more week in this loony bin and then I'm history."

Richards tossed the folder on the desk, turned back to Dan, and furrowed his brow. "Listen to me carefully, Mr.

Coast. Your court-ordered six-week stay with us may be up in a few days, but it takes my signature to secure your release. You might want to keep that in mind next time we meet. Do I make myself clear?"

Dan clenched his jaw for a second, took a deep breath through his teeth, and then replied, "Yeah, I got it." He stood and made his way toward the door.

"From now on we'll be meeting down the hall in *my* office. I'll see you tomorrow, same time," Richards said. "And, Mr. Coast, I'll be taking over the group session this afternoon as well. I look forward to seeing you there, also."

Dan scratched the back of his head with his middle finger as he left the room.

*****

As Dan lumbered down the hall he saw Officer Mel walking toward him at his usual snappy gait. Officer Mel's left arm pointed straight down at his side, and his index and middle fingers were rapidly moving back and forth as he rubbed them together. He gently stroked his own ear with the thumb and index finger of his right hand.

Dan looked up at him as he passed by. Mel was a good four inches taller than Dan and out-weighed him by at least thirty pounds. "Good afternoon, Officer Mel."

Officer Mel stared straight ahead as he passed, tapping the makeshift aluminum foil-covered, cardboard badge that hung around his neck by a piece of pink yarn. "Can't talk, can't talk, can't talk," he explained. "Missing person, missing person. APB, APB."

Ship of Fools

Dan watched Officer Mel make his way down the hall to his room, turn, and disappear through the door. Dan grinned and shook his head. *Crazy bastard.*

"What's Officer Mel's problem this morning, Maxine?" Dan asked at the nurse's station.

A tall, thin woman in blue scrubs stood next to a desk the color of week old puke. Her long fingernails, decorated with monarch butterflies, danced upon a computer keyboard. Maxine was heavy into nail art. All Dan could think about was those cute butterflies passionately raking his bare back.

Maxine turned her head and peered at Dan over her glasses. "What do you mean?"

"He just seems more agitated than usual."

"He gets that way when his sister doesn't show up to visit him for a while." The nurse removed the rubber band from her pony tail and stuck it between her teeth. She combed through her long brown hair with her finger nails and then replaced the rubber band. "When she hasn't been in for a few weeks he starts in with the missing person's shtick."

Dan looked back down the hall toward Officer Mel's room. "How long since she's been in to see him?"

"Why the sudden interest in Mel's sister?"

"Just bored, I guess."

"I'm not really supposed to give out information like that."

Dan looked back toward the maintenance closet behind him. "Really, Maxine?" he asked. "That's where you draw the line?"

Maxine's face flushed and she quickly looked around to make sure no one was within ear shot. "Shhh!"

Dan chuckled. "I'm just saying, after everything we've been through maybe I deserve a little bit of special treatment."

"Everything? That's a bit of an overstatement." she added in a whisper. "Anyway, that quickie in the supply closet *was* your special treatment."

"It was special," Dan agreed.

Maxine was still grinning as her tacky fingernails played the keyboard like a Stradivarius. She stopped typing and began scrolling down the screen. "Here it is. His sister was here three weeks ago yesterday."

"Is that unusual?"

"No, she has gone as much as two months without seeing him at times. I'm sure there's nothing to worry about."

"What does she do for a living?"

Maxine thought for a moment. "I'm not sure; I've only talked to her a few times. It's probably in his file somewhere. You want me to check?"

"No, it doesn't really matter. Maybe I'll have a talk with him, try to calm him down a little."

Maxine turned and opened a file cabinet drawer and began flipping through it. Dan waited patiently at the counter staring at Maxine's perfect ass as she worked.

Maxine turned back. "Is there something else I can do for you, Dan, or are you just enjoying the show?"

"Both," Dan replied. "Great performance but I think it's time for my meds."

Maxine instinctively looked up at the clock and then back at Dan. "Nope. Dr. Richards asked that you be taken off all of your meds, starting today."

"Maybe he's smarter than I gave him credit for." Dan started to walk away but paused. "Maybe next time will be a little *more* special."

Maxine turned. "Next time?"

"Yeah, I don't think those meds were allowing me to performing at my full potential."

"You don't say," Maxine grinned.

"Yeah, so maybe in a few days, you know, just in the name of medical research, we could hit that closet again."

Maxine returned her attention to the file cabinet. "We'll see."

Chapter Two

The smile left Dan's face. "Gone? Gone where? What do you mean?"

"He passed away yesterday afternoon, Mr. Coast. It was his heart."

Dan didn't say a word. He picked up the bike, put it back in the car, and drove away. He took a right off of Atlantic Boulevard on to Bertha Street. When he got to the end of Bertha he pulled to the side of the road and got out of his car. Dan reached under his front seat and grabbed his bottle of tequila in one hand and picked up the bike with the other. Dan walked to the edge of the sidewalk and stood behind the three-foot concrete wall that separated the land from the sea. He set the bike down, opened the bottle, and took a long drink. Setting the bottle on the cement wall, he picked up the bike in both hands, and, as hard as he could, threw it into the ocean.

Dan stood staring quietly out at the horizon as he finished off his bottle of tequila.

When the bottle was empty, Dan sent it flying into the ocean to join the bike.

"Real nice!" came a woman's raspy voice.

Dan turned to see a woman in her late fifties or early sixties walking toward him, hand in hand with a man in his early thirties. They were very tan: she almost blackened, like a gnarled piece of prehistoric driftwood, he more the mocha color of a sun-drenched dog turd.

The man wore white swim trunks with a blue palm tree design and a dark blue Polo shirt; all three buttons were undone and his collar was popped up high. His blond hair was slicked back. Perched upon his peeling nose was a pair Ray-Ban Wayfarers. A diamond stud earring sparkled in his left ear. Dan tried to recall the rule. Right ear: gay. Left ear: straight. Or was it the other way around? This guy looked like he could swing either way.

The woman was in a brown one-piece bathing suit, and over it was a white see-through net dress. Her hair was white and thinner than her boyfriend's. She took a long deep drag on her cigarette, and her lungs rattled as she exhaled. "Real nice!" she repeated. "Throwing garbage into the water like that. It's against the law, you know."

Dan glared at the woman but said nothing.

"There's a garbage can right over there," she said, pointing down Roosevelt Boulevard.

Dan looked at the garbage can and then back at the old hag.

"You have nothing to say for yourself?" she demanded. "What were you thinking?"

Dan had had enough. "I don't know what I *was* thinking. But right *now* I'm thinking that I *shouldn't* have thrown the bottle into the water. I'm thinking maybe I should even swim out there, get the bottle, bring it back here, and then shove it right up your old wrinkled ass."

The old woman grabbed her chest. "Well I never."

Dan looked to her boy toy. "Is that true?"

The young boyfriend reached out and grabbed her arm. "Come along, honey," he purred. "Let's just finish our walk. There's no reason to get into it with this ruffian."

The woman yanked her arm away. "Chad, are you going to let this common trash talk to me like that?"

Chad swallowed hard and stepped toward Dan.

"Don't do it, Chad," Dan warned. "You and the Crypt Keeper just go about your day, and I'll go about mine."

Chad didn't listen; he knew that if he wanted to keep his boy toy status, and all of the perks that went along with it, that this was the time to prove it. He moved closer to Dan.

Dan drew back his hand and slapped Chad across the face, sending him back two steps and knocking his sunglasses to the ground. Chad had a look of total surprise as he rubbed his cheek.

Dan put up his hands in surrender. "Now, Chad, that's how hard I slap__, just imagine how hard I punch."

"Kick his ass, Chad!" the Crypt Keeper hollered.

Chad stepped forward and swung his fist with all of his might at Dan's head. Dan leaned back and the punch missed his nose by half a foot. Chad swung again, this time with his left. Dan leaned back again and again Chad's punch flew wide.

Dan's haymaker smacked Chad's rib cage with a sickening crunch, knocking the wind out of him. Chad staggered back, gasping, and then lunged at Dan, driving him back against the sea wall. Dan winced as his back struck the concrete.

Dan grabbed hold of Chad's shirt with both hands and spun him around. Before he knew what hit him, Dan grabbed the punk's trunks, gave him an atomic wedgie, and hurled him ass over tea kettle over the sea wall and into the sparkling water below.

Dan turned to the old woman. "I warned him."

She ran to the wall, crying. "Why, why?"

Dan climbed back into his Porsche and started the engine. "Because I didn't think he would fit in that garbage can … right over there." Dan turned his car onto Roosevelt and paused only long enough to call out. "Oh, yeah, and Merry Fucking Christmas."

Chapter Three

Dan knocked on the door jamb of Officer Mel's room. Officer Mel looked up from his clip board.

"Can I come in?" Dan asked.

Mel's right hand went instantly to his ear and he began rubbing his earlobe. "My door is always open to the public. Protect and serve, protect and serve, that's my motto." He stood and tossed the clipboard onto the bed. "Make it quick, Dan, I got a lotta paperwork to do. I got a missing person. I got a lotta paperwork."

Dan walked in and took a seat in a lime green chair that matched the wall paint almost exactly. He glanced up at the wall-mounted television directly above him and hoped that maintenance had secured it properly. "That's what I wanted to talk to you about," he said. "I was just wondering if you needed any help on the missing person case."

Mel took a seat in another chair by the window, crossed his legs, and quickly gave Dan a condescending look as well as a chuckle. He tapped his cardboard badge with his finger. "Dan, do you have any idea how long it took me to get this gold shield?"

Dan tried to hide his amusement. "No."

Mel thought for a minute. "I'm not really sure either, but I can tell you it was a long time. I've got a lot of experience in this sort of thing, Dan, and what I don't need is for some second-rate gumshoe wannabe getting in my way."

Ouch, Dan thought. *Second-rate gumshoe? It's bad enough getting ripped a new one by a real cop like Rick Carver, but now I gotta get it from a total whack job. What the Christ!*

"No offense," Mel blurted out.

Dan nodded. "Don't worry about it. I just thought if you needed to talk about anything." When Mel didn't take the bait, Dan got up from the chair and walked toward the door. "Well if you need anything, just yell."

Dan was through the door and into the hall when he heard Mel mumble, "It's my sister."

Dan stopped, leaned back, and looked into the room. "What was that?"

Mel was still sitting in the chair, his elbows on his knees, and cradling his big pumpkin of a head in his hands. "It's my sister that's missing."

Dan came back into the room and sat down. "How long has she been missing?"

"I don't know," Mel responded.

"How long has it been since you saw her?"

Mel squinted his eyes and gazed out the window in thought. "I can't remember."

Dan leaned forward in his chair. "Then how do you know she's missing, Mel?"

"The janitor told me."

"Larry?" Dan asked. "Larry told you your sister was missing?" Dan shook his head and ran his fingers through his hair. He was quickly losing his patience.

"No, it wasn't Larry. It was another guy." Mel pointed at the television. "He came in to fix my TV."

Dan thought for a second. "Had you ever seen this maintenance guy before the day he fixed your TV?"

"No, he said he was new."

"Have you seen him since that day?"

"No."

Dan took a deep breath, held it for a second, and then exhaled. He wanted to choose his words wisely. He knew if Mel started getting confused he would become agitated and shut down. He began speaking slowly. "Okay, Mel, what exactly did the maintenance guy tell you that led you to believe that your sister had been kidnapped?"

"Oh my God." Mel looked worried and confused, his voice was shaky.

"What is it, Mel?"

"Oh my God," Mel repeated. His hands went to his head. "My sister has been kidnapped?" he asked, his eyes crazier than usual.

What the Christ? Dan thought.

Mel leapt from his chair. "My sisters been kidnapped!" he hollered.

Ship of Fools

Dan tried a stern tone. "Officer Mel! Calm down!"

It was too late. Mel had darted out the door and was stalking down the hall, shouting at the top of his lungs, "My sister has been kidnapped, my sister has been kidnapped!"

Dan shook his head and stared at the floor. *I gotta get out of here, these people are nuts.*

Chapter Four

Dan made a U-turn on Roosevelt Boulevard in front of the Sheraton Suites. As he swung a right onto Bertha Street he glanced over at a soaking wet Chad pulling himself over the seawall. His old cougar was not offering any assistance. Chad hollered something, but Dan didn't hear, or care, what it was. Chad threw his middle finger into the air.

Easing the Porsche to the wrong side of the street, Dan came to an abrupt stop in front of the liquor store on Bertha. He pushed open his door and staggered toward the entrance. The tequila he had downed only moments earlier was starting to take effect.

Dan tried to turn the door handle; it didn't budge. He thought of Noah's mother, who couldn't make it to work this morning because her son was dead. Then he noticed the sign someone had made out of a piece of notebook paper and a black marker that had been taped to the door; CLOSED FOR CHRISTMAS. *God dammit*, he thought.

Ship of Fools

He looked up the street in one direction and then back the other. There were no cars; there were no people. It seemed as though Key West had been put on hold for Christmas morning.

Dan raised his foot and kicked in the door, sending shards of splintered door-jamb and glass into the liquor store and across the floor. "Open for business," Dan announced. He wasn't two feet inside the door when the phone began to ring. Dan thought about answering it but instead kept to the task at hand. Moving down the aisle toward the tequila section, he heard the second ring.

Patron? Naw. Cuervo? Naw. Dan grabbed two bottles of the cheap shit, one silver and one gold. He quickly unscrewed the cap of the gold and took a big swig. The phone rang for the fourth time. As he made his way to the checkout counter he thought about Noah, he thought about Noah's mother Jeanie. He remembered her freckles, her dimples, and her smile.

Halfway through the sixth ring Dan heard a click and then a woman's voice coming from an answering machine. *Thank you for calling the Bertha Street Liquor Store. We are closed today for Christmas but will resume our normal hours tomorrow. Thank you and Happy Holidays.*

Dan pulled his money clip from the front pocket of his cargo shorts. He removed a fifty-dollar bill and placed it on the counter. Then looked back at the shattered door and took out four one hundred dollar bills and laid them on top of the fifty.

A man's voice came over the answering machine. *Good morning, this is Southern Most Security. We had an alarm triggered at this address. If someone is there can you please pick up the phone?*

"Shit!" Dan said as he sprinted for his car.

Chapter Five

Dr. Richards sat with his legs crossed and a yellow legal pad resting on his lap. He scribbled away with his number two pencil as Dan stared at him, knowing full well he was probably just drawing pictures of crazy stick people being tortured by fat lazy orderlies.

Look at him, Dan thought, *the captain on a ship of fools. It must be pretty goddamn easy to feel superior in a room full of froot loops.*

Arms folded across his chest, Dan scanned the rest of the loonies in the semi-circle and noticed that Officer Mel had not joined them for Group.

To Dan's right was Lucy Fenton, forty-two, mother of three. Two years ago she found out her husband was having an affair with a young waitress at a little place on Duvall Street. Lucy waited for her husband to leave for work the morning after she discovered his little secret; she never let on that she knew anything about it. But about twenty minutes after he left, she loaded the three kids, ranging in age from three to five, into their brand new mini-van. Witnesses later described the possessed look on Lucy Fenton's face as she barreled down White Street, and proceeded to hop the sidewalk at Atlantic Boulevard, aiming the speeding van and its cargo of her screaming offspring toward the ocean. Thank God no one was injured. Good Samaritans on the beach pulled the scarily calm Lucy and the frantic children from the van as it bobbed like a giant blue cork in the tumbling waves. Lucy's been there ever since, and would be until someone said she wasn't nuts anymore.

Sitting on Dan's left was Billy Maple. He liked to steal things, but if it was too big to steal he just lit it on fire. Billy was the first pyromaniac/kleptomaniac Dan had ever heard of and had recently started referring to him as a klyromaniac. Dan was proud of himself for coining the phrase and hoped it would someday appear in the New England Journal of Medicine.

To Billy's left was an empty chair where Mel usually sat, and to Lucy's right was Mary Timmons, also known as Harry Mary to the group because of her dark facial hair. She sat with a small blanket on her lap.

Mary had been a prostitute in Miami from the time she was fourteen years old until her late thirties, when her pimp decided to throw her out of a moving car because her earnings were on the decline. Mary suffered traumatic brain injury resulting in short-term memory loss. Her long-term memory was also affected in a strange way. She would often put people she now knew into past situations that took place long before she even knew that person. Mary had been talking now for about ten minutes as everyone looked on.

Dr. Richards looked up from his pad when Mary paused to take a breath. "And how did that make you feel, Mary?" he asked.

Dan rolled his eyes.

Mary looked around the group ignoring the doctor's question. Her eyes met Dan's. "Hey, Dan, remember that time in Orlando when we picked up that crack addict, stole his money, and left him on the side of the road in his underwear?"

Dan chuckled. "Yeah, those were good times Mary."

"Dan!" Dr. Richards scolded. "Don't do that. Don't play into Mary's false memories, it confuses her and impedes her progress." He turned his attention back to Mary and in a calm voice said, "Mary, Dan wasn't there. You didn't even know him back then."

Mary began to cry. "Yes, I did. We were friends," she sobbed. Her shoulders began to shake and tears streamed down her cheeks.

Dan shook his head. "Yeah, Doc, your way is much better. Just look at the progress," he said, jerking a thumb at Mary.

Mary pulled the blanket from her lap up over her head and sat silently.

Dan looked on in mingled amusement and pity. "Look, Doc, even *more* progress."

Lucy reached out and began rubbing Mary's back.

"Don't touch me!" came Mary's voice from under the blanket. Lucy quickly pulled her hand back.

"Where's Officer Mel?" Billy asked.

Dr. Richards shot Dan a disgusted look. Dan looked at the ceiling and began to quietly whistle a tune.

"Mel had a little, er, set back this afternoon," Richards answered vaguely. "He was very upset. He'll try to rejoin the group tomorrow."

"Because of his sister's kidnapping?" Billy asked.

"Yeah," Dan said.

"No!" Richards corrected. "Mel's sister has not been kidnapped. She just hasn't been in to see him in a few days, which exacerbates his psychosis."

"Mel told me the janitor kidnapped his sister," Lucy offered.

Billy leaned forward. "No, no, the janitor is the one who *told* him his sister had been kidnapped."

"I heard it was a TV repair man that told him about the kidnapping," Mary said from under the blanket.

"I think it was someone *pretending* to be a TV repair man that told him about the kidnapping," Dan informed the group.

Richards glared at Dan. "That's enough! No one has been kidnapped."

"When's Barbara coming back?" Billy asked.

"She was pretty," came the voice from the blanket. Dan nodded his head in agreement.

"Dr. Morris is not coming back," Richards said.

"Why, what happened?" Lucy asked.

"I bet she was kidnapped!" Billy blurted out.

"I bet she was," Dan laughed.

Dr. Richards slammed his notebook to the tile floor. "No one has been kidnapped! If I hear the word kidnapped out of one more person's mouth, I'm going to … to—"

"Kidnapped," Dan whispered.

Billy laughed out loud. "Kidnapped!" he yelled.

Mary lifted her blanket. "Kidnapped!"

Dr. Richards stood and motioned to a couple of orderlies who began walking toward the group. "I think we're done for today," he said with a heavy sigh.

Dan stood and clapped his hands together. "Now that's progress!"

Chapter Six

Dan had taken a left onto Flagler Avenue and had made it about four blocks before two Key West patrol cars passed him heading the other way. They didn't have their lights on but they were moving a little faster than usual. He looked in his rear view mirror and watched them take a right onto Bertha Street.

Reaching into the passenger seat Dan grabbed the bottle of gold tequila, placed it between his legs, and unscrewed the cap. He took a quick look around to make sure there were no more cops, put the bottle to his lips, and chugged. He placed the bottle back between his legs and reached back into the passenger seat for his sunglasses. He fumbled with the Ray Bans and dropped them into the floor. *Goddammit*. As he leaned over to pick them up he ran the red light at the corner of Flagler and White. The police officer who slammed on his brakes to avoid the collision was not amused and the chase began.

Dan was in the middle of another gulp of tequila when he heard the siren and looked in the mirror to see the flashing lights gaining on him. Dan pushed the accelerator to the floor and grinned.

When Dan refocused on the road ahead it was too late. Flagler Avenue had come to an end and the Porsche was hopping the sidewalk and busting through a small block wall before Dan could hit the brakes. The air bag deployed as the crumpled hunk of fine German engineering side swiped the rear end of a white Ford Bronco, a red Dodge Neon, and a tan Chevy Impala.

Dan yanked the wheel to the right and came to rest against a black Volkswagen Passat. He fought with the air bag as he climbed from the car, his shorts drenched in tequila. He limped around the car, leaned in, and grabbed the bottle of *silver* tequila off of the floor, removed the cap and took a swig.

The police officer brought his cruiser to a stop in the intersection of Flagler and Reynolds, quickly swung open his door, and jumped out.

Dan downed another gulp and smashed the bottle against the door of the car. "Don't come any closer!" he shouted, holding the broken bottle by the neck and brandishing its jagged teeth at the cop.

The officer drew his weapon. "Put it down!" he demanded. Another patrol car skidded to a stop on Reynolds Street, and then another on Seminole.

Dan looked around at the cops. Sweat was stinging his eyes. He took off his sunglasses, threw them to the blacktop, and rubbed the sweat from his brow. He looked at his hand and realized it was blood. He returned his attention to the cop in front of him. "You know who I am?" he screamed. *Wow, did I just say that?*

The door of one of the cruisers swung open and Rick Carver hoisted his portly body out of the seat. The look on his face told Dan that this was not the way Rick had planned on spending his Christmas morning.

Dan waved the broken bottle around with about as much menace as Barney Fife. "I could buy every one of you assholes!"

Rick just shook his head as he kept walking toward Dan, a disgusted look plastered across his face.

"Stay back, you fat piece of shit!" Dan ordered.

Rick pulled his Taser from the holster and aimed as he kept walking. He pulled the trigger and Dan hit the pavement like a two hundred pound sack of shit … mixed with tequila.

Chapter Seven

Dan Coast opened his eyes. He lay face down on his hospital bed, his head turned toward the window. Bright sunlight forced its way through the slats of the closed window blinds. The sound that had awakened him was the bustle of housekeeping cleaning his bathroom. He heard the toilet seat drop and then a flush. He rolled over to see Loretta Farn exiting the bathroom.

"You married, Loretta?" Dan asked.

Loretta wore her silver hair in a bun directly atop of her head. She was a big woman, topping out at least two hundred and sixty pounds. She was sixty-six years old, retired, and cleaned part time at the hospital. "Same man for forty-eight years," she answered, placing the toilet brush in the cleaning cart.

"Oh," Dan said, acting disappointed.

Loretta put her hands on her hips. Her massive bingo wings hung down like two hams in a butcher shop window. "Why do you ask, Coast?" she asked challengingly.

"I was gonna see if I could talk you into getting under these covers with me."

Loretta shook her head. "Coast, if I didn't think it would kill ya, I just might just take you up on that."

Dan chuckled as Loretta pushed her cart out of the room and into the hall. He swung his legs over the side of the bed and slipped his feet into the blue slippers that awaited him and then walked to the window. He took hold of the tilt wand and turned it, opening the blinds. Dan looked out over the horizon and then down at the parking lot where something caught his eye. It was Dr. Richards. Richards seemed to be in an argument with a young woman in her mid-twenties dressed in blue scrubs.

He looks pissed, Dan thought. *She looks pissed too.*

The young woman's face was red and she kept jabbing her finger into Richards' chest. Richards grabbed her arm and pushed it downward. He kept looking around the parking lot and then back at the hospital. He raised his hands in the air and shrugged his shoulders. She swung an open hand at him. He dodged the slap and quickly looked around again.

"I bet that's not *Mrs.* Dr. Richards," Dan whispered to himself with a grin. "What has the good doctor gone and done to get himself into this kind of trouble?"

"Mr. Coast," came a nurse's voice from behind him.

He spun around with a guilty look on his face. "Uh … yes?" he answered.

"What are you doing?"

"Nothing."

The nurse walked into the room and to the window to see what Dan was looking at. "Who are you spying on, Mr. Coast?"

"No one."

She stuck her finger between the slats and separated them to get a better look. "Ha, ha." She removed her finger from the blinds. "Let's get some vitals on you Mr. Coast," she said removing her stethoscope from around her neck.

Dan walked back over and sat on the edge of the bed. "Who was the girl Richards was fighting with, Donna?"

Donna was new at the hospital. She started work the same day Dan arrived, which, in an odd way, made her feel as though she and Dan had about the same seniority, and were learning the ropes together. Other than calling Dan, *Mr.* Coast, she treated him more like he was on the staff rather than one of the patients. Donna was only twenty-one, but with her shoulder-length red hair pulled back in a ponytail, a face full of freckles, and no make-up, she looked more like a volunteer from Key West High. She had just passed her boards two weeks before she was hired and Dan had watched her get scolded by Dr. Richards on more than one occasion.

Donna slid the blood pressure cuff up Dan's arm, and placed the stethoscope's ear tips in her ears. "I probably shouldn't gossip about the staff," She responded, trying her best to sound like a starchy, seasoned nurse.

"But you want to," Dan said with a chuckle.

"Shhh!" she said, listening intently to Dan's heart rate.

Dan remained quiet until she removed the ear tips from her ears. "One-twenty over seventy-nine," she announced. "Much better than the first few days you were here."

Dan rolled his eyes. "So?"

"So, what?"

"So who was the girl arguing with Richards?"

Donna looked around the room. "Her name is Kim Wong."

Dan waited for more. "And?"

"And open your mouth."

Dan did as he was told and Donna shoved a thermometer under his tongue and then grabbed hold of his wrist as she stared at her watch.

Dan's eyes wandered around the room as he waited for Donna to finish the vitals. Under normal circumstances he would just focus his eyes on the nurse's breasts while he waited, trying to get a quick look down her shirt, but with Donna's youthful appearance, that just seemed a little weird, even for Dan Coast. Still, he couldn't help but steal an appreciative glance when she tucked the bell of the stethoscope into her breast pocket. *Lucky bell.*

Donna let go of Dan's wrist, pulled the thermometer from his mouth, looked at it, and then went to the chart holder on the back of the door. Dan's eyes went quickly to her ass out of habit, and then guiltily to the floor. She pulled out the folder, took out her pen, and scribbled something on a piece of paper before returning the folder.

"Am I going to live?" Dan asked jokingly.

"You should make it through the day," Donna shot back.

"So, what else do you have on Kim Wong and the Doc?"

Donna walked back toward Dan. "Well, I don't really know much about her. She's originally from Boston, she's thirty-one, single, and she works on the second floor. Rumor has it that she and Dr. Richards have been seeing each other for about six months. A friend of mine knows her pretty well, and I guess Dr. Richards has been promising to leave his wife for the past couple of months, but Kim is getting sick of waiting and has threatened to go to his wife and tell her about the affair."

Dan raised one eyebrow. "Hmm, I wonder how much gossip I would have gotten if you knew a lot about her?"

"Oh, shut up!" Donna said and slapped Dan on the shoulder.

"Anything else?"

"Well, Loretta, the cleaning lady, said that Dr. Richards has done this before, and that he will never leave his wife because she's the one with all the money. Evidently her family is worth millions and the pre-nup says that if the dastardly doctor leaves her, he gets nothing."

Dan smiled deviously. "Jackpot!"

Chapter Eight

Two officers steered Dan to the holding cell, one hand under each of his sticky armpits. They sat him on a bench at the back of the room, removed the handcuffs, and walked back through the door. He was still staring at the concrete floor when he heard the door slam and the locking mechanism click into position. *Wow, that sounds exactly like it does on television*, he thought.

Dan placed his elbows on his knees and his head in his hands. He wasn't ready to look up yet. He knew the holding cell could be viewed from virtually everywhere in the police station, and he wasn't ready for the judgmental glares that he himself had given to the assholes in whose shoes he now sat.

"Hey!" Dan heard from his left. He ignored it. "Hey!" once again.

"What?" Dan asked, not looking up.

"What did ya do?" the deep voice asked.

"I killed a man for saying 'hey' three times."

"Thank God I only said it twice," came the voice, followed by a chuckle.

Dan lifted his head and leaned his back against the cool block wall behind him. It felt good, and he thought about turning around and pressing his pounding forehead against it. He glanced over at the man seated to his left and did a double take.

The stranger was wearing bright red lipstick that matched his dress and size eleven, six-inch heels perfectly. The dress was skin tight with a slit up to his ass cheek that showed more hairy leg than Dan wanted to see.

"Lola," the man said, extending his hand.

Dan leaned over and shook the man's hand and introduced himself. "Ray Davies," he said.

"Nice to meet you, Ray," Lola replied with a smile.

"What brings a nice girl like you into a place like this?" Dan asked.

Lola brought his hand to the forest of kinky hair spilling out of the plunging neckline of his gown. "I propositioned a police officer."

Dan shook his head. "Yeah, they're pretty hard to spot if they're not wearing a uniform."

"Oh, he was wearing a uniform, honey. But I took a chance anyway. He was just so cute, and he had these sad little eyes, you know, like he needed some of Lola's lovin'."

"And instead of being flattered, he arrested you."

"That's right. You believe he did that?"

"That bastard," Dan said.

Ship of Fools

Lola scooted a little closer to Dan. "Ya know, Ray, you look kinda sad. Maybe *you* could use a little bit of Lola's lovin'."

Dan scooted down the bench, adding a little distance between Lola and himself. "Umm, no. I'm good, thanks anyway," he said nervously.

A voice came at the door just in time. "Come on, Lola, let's go see the judge."

Dan exhaled and leaned his head back against the wall.

Chapter Nine

Dan shuffled down the hallway, along the green and white floor tiles, in his brown hospital-issued slippers. An oak handrail ran along the wall on both sides of the hall. Dan ran his hands along the smooth wood rail as he walked along. The varnish looked brand new, with nary a scrape, scuff, or greasy smudge mark. Dan wondered if anyone ever really used it.

As Dan exited the hallway into the common room his attention went immediately to Officer Mel. Mel, wearing a tan trench coat and a dark gray fedora, held a small notepad in his left hand and a green crayon in his right. He glared menacingly as he looked down at the man seated in front of him.

"Listen, Barney," Mel said. "I'll keep your name out of my report if you cooperate. But if you're going to clam up on me, we'll both take a little trip down town to the station. How would you like that? I'll parade you through the building and let everyone know you're a narc … a snitch, a stoolie."

Ship of Fools

Mel waited for a response but Barney said nothing. He just turned his head and stared out the window into the parking lot. Mel could wait all day. Barney wasn't going to be much help, since he hadn't spoken in about six years.

Dan had snuck a quick peek at Barney Lincoln's file one night while Maxine was on duty. She let Dan look through several files after their encounter in the janitor's closet. As Dan read through the files on those nights, he wondered if Maxine let him read them because she liked him, or if she let him because she was afraid that he might turn her in for the closet sex if she didn't. Dan didn't really care either way, but he never would have told …not anyone at the hospital anyway, but he couldn't wait to tell Red.

Barney Lincoln's file had said that he was once a very wealthy man. Eight years ago he and his wife retired to the Keys and bought a nice house overlooking the gulf. A year later Barney turned on the morning news and found out that the firm he had invested with was being investigated. Barney made call after call that day but there was nothing he could do. He had unknowingly invested heavily in a Ponzi scheme. He and his wife of thirty-five years were broke.

Barney started drinking more and more, and one night, with a foreclosure sign in the front lawn of their dream house Barney and his wife Mavis got into a horrible fight. Barney struck Mavis and she fell backwards hitting her head on a granite countertop. She died in the ambulance on the way to the hospital. Barney hadn't said a word since. He was judged not competent to stand trial and had been at the Lower Keys Behavioral Health Center ever since.

Dan put his hand on Mel's shoulder. "Hey, Mel, why don't you let Barney rest, I don't think he knows anything."

"Listen, Coast," Mel said angrily, jerking his shoulder away. "I don't need some private dick telling me how to do my job. I don't need a partner. I'm a lone wolf, a maverick. Ya got it?"

Dan put up his hands in surrender. "Yeah, yeah, I got it, Mel."

"That's Officer Mel to you, Coast." Mel put the pad and crayon into his shirt pocket and scanned the room. "*Nothing?*" he shouted. Everyone in the room looked up at Mel. "Don't any of you nut jobs have anything to say to me? Someone's missing! And no one saw a thing?"

Dan put both hands on Mel's shoulders. "Calm down, Mel, calm down."

Mel slowly backed up to a chair behind him and sat down. He covered his face with his hands and began to weep. "They're going to kill my sister," he sobbed.

Dan noticed two very large orderlies, Lonnie and Darnell, headed his way. He put up his hand to stop them. "Wait, just wait, he's gonna be okay."

The two men didn't stop. Dan stepped in front of Lonnie.

"Step aside, Coast, if ya know what's good for ya," Lonnie said.

"Just give him a second," Dan said. He grabbed Darnell by the arm.

"Big mistake," Lonnie said with a sick grin that told everyone that he loved his job a little bit too much ...and for the wrong reasons.

Before Dan knew it, he was in a headlock and on the floor with Lonnie on top of him. Lonnie drove his knee into Dan's ribs and leaned into Dan's ear. "I've been waiting for this, smartass," he hissed, and then smashed his knee into Dan's ribs again. "Someone's gotta teach you to keep your nose outta other people's business."

Dan gasped as the air was forced from his lungs. Lonnie's elbow came down on the side of Dan's head. The last thing Dan saw were two orderlies holding Mel down as another stuck a needle into his arm. Lonnie's elbow came down one more time and everything flashed white, and then went dark.

Chapter Ten

Dan Coast sat at a boxy, light oak attorney table with full modesty panels. It reminded him of nothing so much as a coffin. His lawyer, Roland T. Murphy, Esq. was at his left. Across the aisle at a matching coffin was the assistant District Attorney Melvin Cowar. Sitting next to Cowar was another suit that Dan didn't recognize. Everyone had an open briefcase in front of them except for Dan.

Dan turned around and looked over the crowded courthouse. He saw Red and Bev a few rows back. Bev gave a little wave and Red just grinned. Chief Rick Carver stealthily flipped Dan the bird as he shook his head slowly in disgust.

Turning back around and leaning over toward his lawyer, Dan said, "I still think we should fight this."

"Are you stupid?" Roland asked. "I mean, I know you're stupid because if you had any brains at all we wouldn't be sitting here right now."

"Ouch!" Dan replied.

"They've already accepted our plea deal, and you're damn lucky they did. DUI, breaking and entering, petit larceny, unsafe speed while under the influence, fleeing the scene of a crime, resisting arrest, and about eight other charges. Do you know how long they could have put you away for, you goddamn moron? Now just sit there and keep your wise-ass mouth shut. Ya got it?"

Dan slumped back in his chair. "Wow! You're really mean. Do you talk to all of your clients this way?"

"No. I don't have any other clients as ignorant as you."

Dan put his hand on Roland's shoulder. "I'm sensing some hostility, Roland. Do you need a hug?"

Roland shook his head. "Why me?"

The bailiff's voice silenced the room. "Please rise, court is now in session, the Honorable Judge Marjorie Clemons presiding."

The judge looked around the room as she took her seat and the bailiff intoned, "Be seated." Judge Clemens opened a folder on the bench and studied the contents. Without looking up from her paperwork she said, "Mr. District Attorney, I understand that you have reached an agreement with the defense."

"Yes, your honor," Melvin replied.

Clemens looked up at Dan and then at Roland. "And you agree with this most generous deal?" she asked.

Dan nodded his head.

"I'll need a yes from you, Mr. Coast," said Clemens with a slight smirk. "Believe it or not, I can't hear the rocks in your head rattle from there." Several spectators laughed. Dan identified Red's chortle as the loudest. Clemens wrapped her gavel for order.

"Yes, your honor," Dan said somberly.

"Very well, then, Mr. Coast, if you will be so kind as to present yourself at the Lower Keys Behavioral Health Center tomorrow morning at nine o'clock, the great state of Florida will greatly appreciate it … oh, and Mr. Murphy, make sure he gets there or things will get a little sticky, if ya know what I mean."

"Yes, your honor," Roland answered.

Clemens rapped her gavel against the sounding block with satisfaction. "There, that was painless" the judge took a final vulture-to-prey look at Dan, "We're not going to have any more trouble out of you now, are we, Mr. Coast?

"No, your honor," said Dan meekly, adding, "Uh, your honor, if it pleases the court, may I asked a question?"

Too late, Roland saw the telltale twinkle in his mad client's eye.

Clemens sighed. "If you must, Mr. Coast."

"Will the nuthouse supply my straightjacket or should I bring my own?"

Clemens banged her gavel to silence the titters. "Mr. Coast, you wouldn't be taking advantage of the fact I run a fairly informal courtroom to make a mockery of these proceedings"

"No, your honor."

"And I take it you have your own straightjacket?"

"Yes, your honor. Blue. Matches my eyes."

The courtroom erupted in raucous laughter. Clemens let the hilarity play out without banging her gavel and fixed Dan in a glacial stare.

"Mr. Coast." she said in a measured tone. "I walked into that one, and so I'm not going to find you in contempt of court. I will leave you with this: There's nothing funny about mental illness, and while I don't think you, Mr. Coast, are clinically mentally ill, you definitely have a few screws loose, to use the vernacular. It is my hope your stay in this facility will open your eyes to the plight of people with real problems … and perhaps make you finally recognize your own. And one other thing, Mr. Coast."

"Yes, your honor?" Dan said sheepishly.

The shadow of a smile flickered on the judge's face. "Your eyes are brown."

Chapter Eleven

When Dan Coast awoke he was in his room, in his bed, on his back. Maxine was holding his wrist as she gazed at her watch, and Dr. Richards stood at the foot of his bed.

"I hear you had a little accident, Mr. Coast," Richards said.

Maxine let go of Dan's arm. "Got quite a bump on your head there."

Dan turned his attention to Dr. Richards. "An accident?" he asked groggily.

"Lonnie said you tried to help Mel, and you tripped and fell and hit your head on the floor."

Dan lifted his hand, rubbed the lump over his left eye and winced.

"I'll get you an ice pack for that," Maxine said.

"Thanks," Dan replied.

Ship of Fools

Dr. Richards prepared to exit. "I'll stop back in a few hours and check in on you, Mr. Coast." Richards turned as he got to the door. "Maxine, let's check in on Mr. Coast every half hour until around two in the morning. With that concussion I don't want him falling asleep right away."

"Yes, Dr. Richards."

"Yes, Dr. Richards," Dan mocked after the doctor left the room. Maxine playfully stuck out her tongue at him. "How old are we?" Dan observed. "Five?"

"Just about," said Maxine. "Be right back."

Maxine left the room and returned a few minutes later with the ice pack. "Here, put this on your forehead for a little bit. It will help with the swelling."

"Thanks, Maxine." Dan winced as he laid the pack on his wound.

Maxine grabbed the remote control off of the night stand and pointed it at the television. "So what happened? Did you trip, or slip on the floor?"

"Neither," Dan replied.

"What do you mean?" Maxine flipped through the channels.

"That fat piece of shit, Lonnie, bounced my head off the floor on purpose and then smashed his elbow into my temple a few times with a couple of knees to the ribs for good measure."

"Are you kidding me?"

"Does this lump on my head look like a joke?" Dan glanced out the window and noticed it was still daylight. "How long was I out?'

Maxine looked at the clock again, it was three o'clock. "Only about fifteen minutes," she replied.

Dan adjusted the ice pack. "It seemed longer."

Maxine walked over and lifted the ice pack. "It wasn't that bad, the swelling is already going down."

Dan focused on the TV. Maxine was still holding the remote control and had stopped on an episode of *Roseanne*. "Over my dead body," Dan protested.

"Don't tempt me," said Maxine. She resumed channel surfing and stopped on *The Montel Williams Show*.

"Oh, shit, just give me the remote," Dan groaned.

He switched channels until he came to an old *Remington Steele* episode from the late eighties. He put the remote back on the nightstand and clasped his fingers behind his head.

"Oh, I remember this show, my Dad used to watch it when I was a little kid," Maxine recalled. "That Pierce Brosnan was a hottie back then. Now he's an old man. Older than you, even."

Dan just stared at the TV. "Swell."

Chapter Twelve

When Dan awoke the only thing that lit his room was the television. Someone had turned it down at some point. He turned his head toward the window and gazed out at the blackness of night. The blinking red light of a sailboat's mast, way off in the distance, caught his eye. Rolling over to the other side of the bed Dan placed his feet on the cold floor and fumbled for his slippers. Not finding them he stood and made his way to the bathroom and flipped on the light.

He turned on the cold water and splashed a couple of handfuls on his face and then one over his head and through his hair. He grabbed a towel and dried his face as he stared at himself in the mirror. He liked what he saw. These last few weeks without a drink had taken a few years off of his face. The whites of his eyes were whiter and the tiny red veins that occupied them were almost non-existent. *Wow*, he thought, *I didn't realize how bad I looked before*. He shook his head and tossed the towel back on the towel bar. It missed and fell to the floor. He left it where it landed.

The light from the bathroom flooded Dan's room. He bent down and looked under his bed for the slippers. *What the Christ?* he thought. *I bet they're out in the common room.*

Dan walked to his door and poked his head out into the hallway. He could see the nurses station from his room but there was no one there. He stepped out into the hall and looked past the common room into the other wing. Officer Mel's light was on and Dan could see shadows, on the floor of the hall, coming from Mel's room. *What's going on down there?*

Dan quietly made his way down the hall, past the nurses station, through the common room and into the hallway that led to Mel's. As he got closer he could hear the mumble of voices but couldn't make out what was being said. Out of caution he began to tiptoe.

When he got to Mel's open door he looked in. Mel was sitting on the edge of his bed in his red, one-piece, feety-pajamas, his cardboard badge dangling from his neck. Lonnie stood with his back to the door, his arms folded in front of him. Another man, tall, with thick, black, slicked back hair stood in front of Mel. The unknown man was muscular and hunched slightly. He slammed his big meaty fist into the palm of his hand, and when it smacked Mel flinched.

Lonnie spoke calm and quietly. "Officer Mel, just tell him what he wants to know and then he'll leave you alone."

Mel's eyes went from the goon to Lonnie and he slowly shook his head no. "Can you call my sister please, Lonnie?" Mel asked. His voice was soft and shaky.

"Mel, I told you, I don't know where your sister is. If you want her to be okay, though, you have to answer Manny's questions."

Manny was growing impatient. He jabbed a finger at Mel. "Listen, ya goddamn retard, if ya don't start spillin' your guts, I'm gonna spill 'em for ya, ya got it?"

Dan had heard enough and stepped quietly into the room. "Hey, asshole, we don't use that word here."

Lonnie spun around and only got out the word "Coast" as Dan's foot swiftly rose up to crush his testicles. Lonnie dropped to his knees and slumped over holding his package and moaning.

Mel jumped to his feet and stood on his bed, pointing at Lonnie. "One-Adam-twelve!" he shouted. "One-Adam-twelve. Two-eleven in progress. Handle code three, handle code three!"

The big man reached into his jacket. Dan knew he was going for a gun. He lunged at the man, grabbing his right hand. Dan felt the cold steel of the gun's barrel and fought to keep it pointed away from him. The two men tumbled on to Mel's bed and then rolled to the floor.

"Officer down, officer down!" Mel screamed.

"Go get help!" Dan hollered, as Manny drove a left into Dan's ribs and then his shoulder.

Mel put one hand over his ear and the other he used as a microphone. "Rampart, this is squad fifty-one. We got a man down. He appears to be in his early thirties."

Out of the corner of his eye, Dan could see Lonnie crawling out of the door. "Mel, help!" Dan screamed.

As Mel jumped up and down on his bed he shouted orders: "Ringers lactate! Fifty cc's of D5W!"

Manny grunted, pulling the gun from his jacket. Both of Manny's hands, as well as both of Dan's were on the gun.

With every bit of his strength Dan smashed Manny's hands against the leg of Mel's bed once, twice, and on the third time the gun flew from Manny's hands and slid under the bed and against the wall.

"Get the gun, Mel!" Dan shouted.

Mel shouted back, "I've been the sheriff of Mayberry for a long time, Dan, and I've never carried a gun."

What the Christ? Dan crawled toward the gun on his belly, pulling himself with his palms and pushing with his toes. He reached out and grabbed the gun. Manny was up and heading toward the door.

Dan rolled out from underneath the bed and jumped to his feet. When he got to the hall he heard the door to the stairway slam shut. Manny and Lonnie were both gone. *Dammit!*

Dan ejected the clip from the 9mm, and then, yanking back the slide, he emptied the last shell from the chamber. He picked up the shell and went to the wall cabinet. Opening the door, he reached inside and grabbed two rubber gloves. He placed the pistol in one and the ammunition in the other and tied a knot in the end of each glove. Dan then walked into Mel's bathroom and removed the lid from the toilet tank. He placed each glove in the water and replaced the lid.

Dan was exiting the bathroom as a nurse burst into Mel's room. "What's going on in here," she demanded, looking around the disordered room.

"Call the police," Dan said.

Mel leapt from the bed. "No need. I'm on the job," he said tapping his badge.

Chapter Thirteen

Chief of Police Rick Carver, beefy arms folded across his fat dune of a belly, leaned against the wall of the common area near the nurses station. He usually removed his gold-rimmed aviator sun glasses when he was indoors, but not today.

Dan was giving his statement to another cop, Officer Tim Shackley. Shackley repeatedly looked from his note pad to Dan and then back as he jotted. Dan looked back and forth from Shackley to Rick. Rick never shook his head or gave any other indication that he was even listening to Dan.

"Manny, that's with a Y, right?" Shackley asked.

"He didn't have a name tag but I would assume so," Dan replied.

"What was he wearing?" Officer Mel asked.

Dan turned to see Mel leaning against the nurses station, note pad in hand.

"Mel, you were right there with me," Dan replied, shaking his head. "You know what he was wearing."

Shackley interrupted. "Mr. Coast, the orderly"—he checked his notes—"Lonnie, did he lay a hand on either you or Mel?"

"That's *Officer* Mel," Mel said in an authoritative voice.

"No," Dan responded. "Not then."

Shackley looked up from his pad. "What do you mean, 'Not then'?"

"Well, earlier in the day I got into it with him."

"Got into it?"

Dan rolled his eyes. "He and another orderly tried to sedate Mel"—Dan put up his hand quickly—"I mean *Officer* Mel."

"And what did that have to do with you?"

Rick Carver cleared his throat and spoke for the first time. "Mr. Coast has a nasty habit of sticking his nose into other people's business."

All eyes went to Rick, and Dan wished he wasn't wearing his corny shades. It's hard to get a read on someone when you can't see their eyes. However, Dan *could* see the muscles on Rick's face bulge as he clenched his jaw. *Wow, he's really pissed this time*, Dan thought.

"The orderlies were the ones who got Officer Mel riled up," Dan explained. "I just wanted the chance to try and calm him down before they started jabbing needles into his arm. When I stepped in front of Lonnie, he tackled me and smashed my head against the floor."

Shackley closed his pad. "So, you were looking to get even when you kicked him in the balls."

Dan shook his head. "What the Christ?"

Shackley looked at the nurse. "You were on duty, ma'am. Did you witness any of this?"

The nurse looked up from her battered copy of *The Globe*. "I didn't see anybody but these two. Lonnie's shift ended at eleven, so I don't know what he would have been doin' here at this time of night anyways."

Shackley's eyes went to Mel. "Officer Mel, do you think these guys were here to hurt you?"

"That other guy did have a gun."

Dan's head whipped around and his eyes met Mel's.

"A gun?" Shackley asked.

Dan glared at Mel.

"A gun?" Mel asked. "Did I say a gun? What I meant to say was, he had something that *looked* like a gun. But it was definitely not a gun …or a knife …or any other kind of a weapon that could be used to hurt someone. It was probably a Heath bar … or Skor. I like Heath bars better than Skor, so it was probably a Heath bar." Mel's eyes shot toward the ceiling; he was suddenly in deep thought. "Do they still make Sky Bars?"

Shackley rolled his eyes and placed his notepad back in his belt and his pen back in his shirt pocket.

Rick pushed his hefty frame away from the wall with a faint grunt. "Shackley, you can head on back down stairs."

"So that's it?" Dan asked. "Case closed?"

Rick watched as Shackley walked down the hall and onto the elevator and then turned to Dan. "Listen, Coast, I don't expect to get called down here again. Ya got it?"

"But, Rick—,"

Rick threw up a hand in Dan's face and then said to the nurse, "I'll have a man walk around the building a few times and have a unit drive by till morning. If you see anyone suspicious, give me a call. But don't let this man near a phone, because if I get a call from him there's gonna to be trouble."

The nurse smiled. "Thanks, Chief."

As Rick walked away Dan said, "Rick." The chief paused with his back to Dan. "Rick, I'm sorry about the fat bastard remark."

"It was 'fat piece of shit,'" Rick corrected, and went on down the hall.

Chapter Fourteen

When Dan awoke for the second time in one day, the sun was shining though the partially closed blinds. He looked to the bathroom and could tell by the way the towel hung on the rod that Loretta, the housekeeper, had already made her rounds. He was a little disappointed he missed her and their early morning banter.

He jumped out of bed, slid his feet into his slippers, and went to the bathroom to shit, shower, and shave, and whatever else needed to be done to start the day. When he finished he went to the window, opened the blinds, and stared out into the parking lot. He wondered what kind of car Dr. Richards drove. Then he wondered what kind of car Kim Wong drove. He wondered if they were both already in the building. Did they have another fight before work? Then he thought about Mrs. McGee, his across-the-street neighbor, and how many times he had caught her with her nose hanging out her front window, watching the comings and goings of the neighborhood.

Holy shit! he thought as he turned from the window. *I'm turning into Edna McGee. I gotta get outta this place.*

Dan left his room and walked to the nurses station. "Whassup, Maxine?"

Maxine looked up from the computer screen and gave Dan a head to toe scan, apparently liking the improvement. "You look nice. And you don't smell like a goat, for a change."

"Uh, thanks. I think. Is Dr. Richards in?"

"He is, but he was called downstairs about ten minutes ago. Something about the little commotion that went on here last night."

"It was early this morning," Dan corrected, staring down the hall toward Dr. Richards office.

"Night, morning, whatever. What happened, anyway?"

Dan ignored the question. "Did Lonnie show up for work this morning?"

Maxine looked up at the schedule that hung on the wall above her. "No," she shook her head. "He's off Thursdays all month."

"Mel up yet?"

"He already went down to the cafeteria for breakfast."

"You said Richards went downstairs about ten minutes ago?"

"Yeah. Why?"

Dan shrugged his shoulders. "Just wondered."

Dan left the nurses station and went into the common room. He looked around the room and spotted a CD lying on a table next to the radio. He quickly made his way to the CD, picked it up, and walked down the hall to Dr. Richards' office, which was across the hall from Mel's room. He looked back down the hall to make sure no one was watching and then slid the CD between the door jamb and the door stop. *Click.* He pushed the door open and went in.

While taking a quick scan of the office, Dan immediately went for the desk. Lying face down behind a wooden nameplate was just what he was looking for; Richards' cell phone, which Dan knew the good doctor seldom kept on his person in a nod to professional etiquette. He picked it up, turned it over, and pressed the little button on the side and the cell lit up. He swiped his index finger across the face and it opened. *What a moron,* Dan thought. *No pass code on your phone? Any idiot could get any information they wanted... and one is about to.* Dan smiled big as he removed the back plate and then the SIM card. A recovering Luddite, Dan had finally decided, with Red's help, to embrace technology and learn about workings of the infernal contraptions that allegedly made life easier.

Dan quietly opened Richards' door and peered into the hall. Richards was at the nurses station, his back to Dan. He was flirting with Maxine. *Good luck, asshole, it took me two weeks to get her into that closet.* Dan stuck his arm into the hall and waved his hand at Maxine. Maxine's eyes widened when she saw it. He pointed at Richards and then down the hall.

Maxine quickly stuck up her wait-a-minute finger and then turned and grabbed a chart off of the desk behind her. She pointed down the hall and started walking in that direction. Dr. Richards followed closely behind. If he was on all fours his tail would have been wagging and his nose would have been buried in her butt.

Dan watched until they disappeared around the corner and then exited Richards' office. As he walked past Mel's room he peeked inside. Knowing Mel was still at breakfast, Dan went into his bathroom and retrieved the pistol from the toilet tank. He removed each item from its rubber glove, tossed the gloves in the waste basket, shoved the clip up into the grip, and, lastly, placed the gun in the back of his waistband.

"Good morning, Mr. Coast," Dan heard as he entered the hallway from Mel's room, still adjusting his shirt tail.

Dan looked up to see Dr. Richards headed his way. "Good morning, Sigmund," Dan replied.

"I hear we had a little commotion here last night."

"Golly gee, *we* certainly did. But it was this morning."

Richards sneered. "Whatever time it was, I hear the authorities were called."

"No, just the police," Dan responded.

"And what seemed to be the problem?"

Dan continued to walk past Richards. "I'm sure it's all in the police report, Sigmund. Why don't you request a copy from *the authorities*, and read all about it yourself."

Richards stopped in the hall and slowly turned as Dan walked by. "Oh, don't worry, Mr. Coast, that's just what I intend to do."

Dan grinned. "I'm not worried, Sigmund, but thanks for your concern."

Chapter Fifteen

"I'm gonna leave this place today, Officer Mel. Do you want to come with me?" Dan asked.

Mel sat across the white Formica banquet table devouring the last few bites of his scrambled eggs, toast, and sausage.

He slowly lifted his head. "They won't let me leave."

Dan looked around the room. "I have a plan to get myself out of here, and if you want I can take you with me."

A smile blossomed on Mel's kisser. "We're gonna escape?"

"No, we're not going to escape. Dr. Richards is going to sign me out, and I can take you with me. I'll help you find your sister." Dan sipped his coffee from the white porcelain mug.

Mel scanned the room and whispered, "Yes, I want to get out of here." He thought for a moment. "They keep all of the windows and doors locked. We'll need to steal someone's key card to open the door at the end of my hall that leads to the stairway. Swiping the key card will keep the alarm from sounding. When we get to the ground floor we'll want to take a right instead of exiting through the side door. There's a security camera on the side door. We'll walk down the hall and take the first right that leads to the laundry room. We'll grab two pairs of scrubs, go into the bathroom, and put them on. Then it's through the laundry room, out the door, through the parking lot, across the street and boom, we're at Kmart. All we gotta do is call a cab and we're home free. If we leave right after lunch no one will miss us for about two hours."

When Mel finished he sat quietly staring at Dan, breathless, a big grin on his face, and his head going up and down like a bobblehead toy.

Wow! Dan thought. *This guy has thought about this for quite some time. And his toolbox is not short a screwdriver after all.* "Mel, I told you we weren't going to escape. Dr. Richards is going to let us leave."

Mel looked disappointed. "But I wanted to escape."

"But we don't have to."

Mel started rubbing his ear and his fingers started twitching. "I think it's a good plan."

"Okay, okay, calm down, Mel," Dan said, placing his hand on top of Mel's. "We'll do it your way, but how about if I have a friend of mine pick us up at Kmart instead of calling a cab?"

"Great idea …can we trust him?"

"Yes, we can trust him."

Mel took one more look around the cafeteria. "Let's talk firepower."

"Firepower?"

"Check, firepower. I've got the gun in my toilet but we're gonna need one for you and a couple shotguns, 12gauge will be fine. I think we will also need an AR-15, and two or three hand grenades each."

Dan gulped "That's an awful lot of firepower, Mel."

"You never know what we're getting ourselves into."

"Funny, I was just thinking the same thing."

"So, we're on the same page?"

"I don't even think we're in the same book, Mel. The one gun is enough for now. We don't want to call a lot of attention to ourselves. Ya know what I mean?"

Mel looked confused. "Not really, but I trust you, Dan. Should we synchronize our watches?"

"I don't wear a watch, Mel, and neither do you."

Mel slid his empty breakfast tray to the side and stood. "Okay then, I'll see you after lunch, Dan." Mel gave an over-animated wink and headed for the door.

What the Christ am *I getting myself into?*

Chapter Sixteen

"Dan, you know you're only supposed to have your phone from noon to three on Sundays."

"Is that some kind of state law, Maxine, or is it just your ... *policy*?" Dan replied, making finger quotes as he said the word policy.

Maxine rolled her eyes. "Exactly, it's our policy."

"COAST!"

They heard Dr. Richards' voice echo from somewhere on the floor.

"Shit!" Dan said, quickly reaching into his pocket and pulling out the SIM card he had taken from Dr. Richards' cell phone. "Take this, Maxine, and don't give it to Richards no matter what."

Maxine shoved the card into the pocket of her blue scrubs. "What is it?"

"It's my ticket out of here. Guard it with your life— I owe you big."

Maxine flashed an evil smile. "How big?"

"Maxine, please."

Dr. Richards rounded the corner into Dan's room. "What's going on in here?" he asked.

Maxine removed the stethoscope from around her neck. "I was about to take Mr. Coast's vitals one last time."

Richards glared at Dan. "There's no need. He's fine, Maxine. Can you leave us alone for a minute?"

"Sure Doctor," she replied, returning the stethoscope to its resting place.

"Close the door on your way out."

"Yes, Doctor." Maxine pulled the door closed behind her.

"Is there a problem, Sigmund?" Dan asked, faking his deepest concern.

Richards looked back at the door to make sure Maxine was gone and then around the room as if he was searching for something. He stepped closer to Dan. "Something is missing from my office, Coast."

"Well, thanks for letting me know. Can you describe the missing item for me so I can keep an eye out for it?"

Richards' face reddened and he hissed through gritted teeth. "You have a smart mouth, Coast."

"I prefer to think of it as a razor sharp wit."

"I can make things pretty tough on you in here."

"I doubt it," Dan said and turned toward the window. He walked across the floor and peered out into the parking lot. "If you feel what's missing is in my room, feel free to look around. If not, get the hell out."

Richards took one last look around the room and headed toward the door. "This isn't over, Coast!"

Dan grinned as he stared out the window. "You got that right, Sigmund," he whispered.

When Dan heard the door shut behind him he went to his bed and climbed in on top of the blankets. He adjusted the pillows between his back and the headboard, and crossed his stretched out legs in front of him. He grabbed the remote control, turned on the television, and flipped through the stations, stopping on *The Price Is Right*. He never thought anybody could replace Bob Barker, but the dude was older than dirt, and Drew Carey was growing on him … and the models were more bodacious than ever. As George Gray called another contestant to come down, Dan pushed the call button.

"Nurses station," came Maxine's voice from the small speaker. "What is it, Dan?"

Dan folded his fingers behind his head and leaned back against the head board as he watched the Plinko chip bounce from pin to pin. "Maxine, can you come in here for a minute, please? I need your help with a little project I'm working on."

"Ugh, I'll be right there."

Dan adjusted the volume and then shouted, "One hundred and ninety-nine dollars!"

And then Drew said, "The actual retail price is … three hundred and forty-five dollars."

"For a goddamn blender?"

The door opened. "Can you come in here for a minute?" Maxine asked, mocking Dan. "Ya know, I'm your nurse, not your secretary."

"So … no *dick*-tation?" Dan said with a leer.

"Ha, ha, very funny."

"Did Richards say anything to you after he left my room?" Dan asked.

"No. He didn't even look at me. He's really pissed."

Dan chuckled. "I would imagine." He held out his hand. "The chip."

Maxine retrieved the SIM card from her pocket. "So, what are your plans for this thing?" she asked placing it in the palm of Dan's hand.

"You'll see," he replied, holding out his other hand. "Cell phone."

Maxine furrowed her brow. "*My* cell phone?"

"Yup."

She rolled her eyes, took her phone out of her other pocket, and handed it to Dan. "This better not come back on me."

Dan removed the back of her phone, took out her SIM card and replaced it with the good doctor's. He stared at the screen for a few seconds and then handed it back to Maxine. "Your phone's different than mine. How do I see what's on Richards' card?"

"Here, hand it over," said Maxine.

He watched as she tapped the screen a few times and then swiped her finger across it. About the fourth time she swiped, her eyes widened. "I would assume this is what you're looking for." She turned the phone to show Dan a picture of a beautiful Asian woman, the same woman Richards had been arguing with in the parking lot. She stood in a bathroom, wearing nothing but duck lips as she snapped a selfie nudie with her cell phone.

Dan nodded appreciatively and reached for the phone. "Bingo!" He flipped from one picture to the next. He found about six photos of the woman, and then he came to one photo of Dr. Richards and the same young woman lying side by side in bed, gloriously nekkid. Richards was holding his phone and pointing it toward the mirror on the ceiling above them. Dan grinned. "Bingo again!"

Chapter Seventeen

It was a little after one when Dan made his way through the common room and down the hall toward Richards' office door. He came to Mel's room first. Mel sat patiently on his bed. He was wearing black dress pants, a white button-down shirt, a black tie, and a black jacket. Mel's hair was neatly combed to the side. Dan looked down at the suitcase sitting in the middle of Mel's floor.

"Ready?" Mel asked eagerly

Dan put up his hand. "Keep your pants on, Mulder. I gotta run in and talk to Dr. Richards for a minute."

Mel looked down at his pants. "Okay."

Dan turned the doorknob and went in without knocking. Richards looked up at the clock on the wall.

"Group isn't for another hour, Coast," he said disgustedly and returned his attention to the papers on his desk.

Dan closed the door behind him, walked to the nearest chair and sat. "I just have a quick question, Sigmund and then I'll be out of you long, luxurious hair."

Richards laid down his pen. "What is it, Coast? I have a lot of paperwork to do."

"Hypothetically speaking, when I get out of here, do you have the authority to release another patient into my care?"

Richards shook his head. "Okay, Coast, I'll play. Sure, hypothetically speaking I do have the authority, as long as the patient is here voluntarily and not by an order of the court. Why do you ask?"

"Because I'm leaving today, and I would like to take Mel with me."

"Mel Gormin?"

"Yes."

Richards snickered. "You're not going anywhere, Coast, and I wouldn't trust you to watch my dog, much less be responsible for Mel Gormin. Now if you don't mind, like I said, I have a lot of work to do. I'll see you in Group." He picked up his pen and began writing.

Dan leaned over in his chair and pulled a folded piece of white computer paper from his front pocket. "I'm leaving, Sigmund, and this is my ticket," he said, tossing the paper onto Richards' desk.

Richards froze and stared at the paper for a few seconds before picking it up. "What's this?" he asked as he slowly unfolded it.

"Well," Dan replied, "I could sugarcoat it, make it sound a little nicer than it is, but when it's all said and done, its blackmail."

Ship of Fools

A vein running down the middle of Richards' forehead bulged, his face reddened, and his jaw clenched. "I knew it was you," he said through his teeth.

Dan leaned back in the chair and put his feet up on the desk. "Calm down, Sigmund, you look like you're gonna stroke out. You have nothing to worry about. No one but you and I and Ms. Wong will ever see that picture … or any of the others I sent to my email."

Richards let the paper drop on the desk. "I have a wife."

"Well, yeah, Sigmund." Dan smiled. "If ya didn't this whole blackmail thing wouldn't work, now would it?"

"You're a real bastard, Coast."

"I never said I wasn't, but I'm not the one in that photo at the No-Tell Motel with my winky in the Wong girl. Get it … the Wong girl?"

Richards wasn't amused.

Dan waved his hand around the room. "Now sign whatever papers ya gotta sign to get me and Mel outta here and I'll be out of your hair for good."

Richards glanced over at his file cabinet. "Okay, Coast, but how do I know, once you're out of here, you won't show these to my wife anyway?"

"You don't."

Chapter Eighteen

It only took Dr. Richards about an hour to make the calls he had to make and to fill out the appropriate paperwork he had to fill out for Dan's release—and Mel's temporary release— into his custody.

Dan leaned against the nurses station, chatting with Maxine as Richards walked down the hall toward him. Richards handed Dan a file folder. Dan stuck out his hand to shake. Richards ignored the gesture. Maxine turned and went back to her work.

"Just leave," Richards said.

Dan peered over Richards' shoulder. He could see Mel peeking out of his doorway. "Gladly, Sigmund, gladly, but I need one more favor."

"Of course you do."

"Mel wants to escape."

Richards looked confused. "Escape?"

"Yeah. It seems he's been planning an escape for quite a while and he wants to carry it out today."

"But I filled out all of the paperwork! He doesn't have to escape."

"I know that and you know that, but things will go a lot smoother if we just play along."

Richards turned back toward his office and mumbled, "Whatever."

"I don't think he likes me," Dan said, turning back to Maxine, who had just returned to the counter with a large clear Zip-loc bag.

Maxine un-zipped the bag and removed two prescription bottles. Holding up the first one she said, "Give Mel one of these every six hours with food." She then held up the other. "And these are very important. Give him one pill twice a day, also with food."

"Why are *those* so important?"

"In layman's terms, they keep him from going crazy."

"Holy shit! He can get crazier?"

"He could."

"What the Christ?" Dan said, looking down the hall. Mel was now standing in the hall, suitcase in hand. Dan held up ten fingers and whispered loudly, "Give me ten minutes."

Mel grinned, winked, and nodded his head.

Dan took the Zip-loc bag from Maxine and started down the hall. Midway, he paused and looked back. "I don't have to wipe his ass or anything, do I?"

Maxine grinned. "Only if you want to."

*****

Dan jammed the last of his clothing, along with the pistol he had acquired from Manny, Mel's pills, and three pairs of flip-flops into his small blue duffle bag. A fourth pair of flip-flops he dropped to the floor and slid in his feet. *Ahhhh,* he thought. He zipped up the duffle bag and took one last look around the room. "I won't miss this place," he whispered before turning and leaving.

"Ready to go?" Dan called out to Mel as he walked down the hall toward him.

Mel put his shush finger to his lips and nodded toward the door. He turned and Dan followed, shaking his head.

The two escapees were through the door and down the stairs in no time. As they entered the corridor to the laundry room, Mel pressed his back up against the wall. He then pointed at himself, pointed down the hall, let his fingers do the walking through the air, and then pointed at his own eyes. Dan shrugged.

"I'm going to go have a look in the laundry room, make sure the coast is clear," Mel explained.

"I knew that," Dan responded.

Mel tiptoed down the hall, hugging the wall all the way. When he came to the door he peeked through the side light into the laundry room. When he was satisfied the room was empty, he waved Dan in.

Once inside Mel went directly to a shelf on the far wall. He grabbed a pair of scrubs and tossed them to Dan. "Put these on," he said. "We don't want to look suspicious."

"I think that ship sailed," Dan replied.

"Just put them on."

Dan did as he was told, putting on the scrubs over his clothing, and Mel did the same. Mel pulled two stethoscopes from the side pouch of his suitcase and handed one to Dan.

"What's this for?" Dan asked.

"Put it around your neck like this." Mel demonstrated. Dan once again complied.

Dan pushed the back door open and the glare hurt his eyes. But he felt the sun's warmth on his face and smiled. He was glad to be outside—for good.

The two men walked through the door, across the rear parking lot, down Twelfth Street, and into the Kmart parking lot.

"What does your friend drive?" Mel asked, scanning the parking lot.

Dan shrugged. "Who knows?" he said, and began removing his scrubs. "Are you gonna take those off?"

Mel looked down at his outfit. "I think I'll keep mine on."

"Listen, Mel, I don't want you telling anyone you're a cop. Alright?"

"Why not?"

Dan thought for a second. "We're gonna work this case undercover. We don't want the local cops thinking that some rogue cop and his PI sidekick are nosing around in their business."

Mel nodded and grinned. "Good idea, Dan."

A gold 1975, Firebird pulled up in front of them and the window lowered. "Whaddaya think?" Red asked, grinning from ear to ear. "It's just like Rockford's. I got it off Craigslist."

"Were they fresh out of Batmobiles?" Dan asked.

"You are so goddamn jealous," Red shot back.

Dan looked the car over. "You're right, this is pretty cool."

"Who's your friend?" Red asked.

"This is Me—"

Mel threw up a hand to quiet Dan and stuck his other hand through the window of Red's car. "I'm Dr. John McIntyre. I'm assisting Dan in a case he's working on."

Accustomed to surrealism as a longtime pal of Dan's, Red took Mel's odd introduction in stride and shook his hand. Without missing a beat, he said, "Nice to meet you, Trapper, jump in."

Dan walked around the back of the car as Mel hurried around the front.

"Shotgun!" Mel hollered.

Chapter Nineteen

Red took a right onto Kennedy Drive and then hung a right onto Flagler Avenue. As they drove past Eleventh Street Dan looked back at the small block house that sat on the corner of Eleventh and Riviera. He thought about the shootout with Milton Guff, he thought about Noah, and Noah's mom, Jeanie. He wondered if Jeanie had to clean up the mess he made at the liquor store. *I need a drink,* he thought.

"Where to?" Red asked.

"Your place," Dan answered.

"My house?"

"Your bar," Dan corrected.

"You don't want to head home first?"

"Why?"

"I dunno… to see your dog."

"Yeah, I bet that damn dog really missed me. Who's been looking in on him while I was… away?"

"Bev had him the first few days, and then Cindy and Derrick took him over to their place."

"Cindy and Derrick are finally back home, huh?"

"Yeah, they got back a few days after ya went in. Cindy's back at the bar, but tonight is her night off, and Phil asked Derrick to come back to Island Adventures. He really needed the help after he got out of the hospital."

"How *is* Phil doing?"

"Real good. He's still going to physical therapy twice a week."

Mel jumped in. "If you ladies are finished catching up on all of the local gossip, maybe we should come up with a game plan on how to find my sister."

"Sister?" Red asked. "What's he talking about?"

Dan explained. "I'm gonna help Dr. McIntyre, here, find his sister. She hasn't been seen in a few weeks and he thinks something may have happened to her."

Dan proceeded to tell Red the whole story about Mel, his sister, and their little run-in with Lonnie and Manny. He even told Red about his little involvement in the blackmail of Dr. Richards that led to his early release. He was just finishing up the story as they pulled into the parking lot of Red's Bar and Grill.

Red's only comment to the story was, "Who's Mel?"

Mel swung open his door and climbed out, shutting the door behind him.

"Forget something?" Dan hollered from the back seat.

Mel ignored him and, like a man on a mission, sprinted across the parking lot for the front door. Red pulled the seat release button and let Dan out of his side.

Dan groaned as he climbed from the back seat. "You might want to think about a four door next time."

"Next time? I think I'm gonna have this baby for a while so you better get used to her."

"You've had six vehicles since I met you and you said the same thing about all of them."

The two men walked across the crushed stone of the parking lot Dan squinted as he stared up at the sun and wiped the sweat from his brow. "You forget how bright and how hot it is out here when you're stuck inside for a few weeks with the air conditioning on."

"I wouldn't know. I'm not stupid enough to get myself into that kind of trouble," Red replied. "And who the hell is Mel?"

Dan walked up the steps and pulled the front door open, letting Red walk in first. "Trapper John's real name is Mel Gormin."

"Ah!"

Dan walked across the wooden plank floor and looked around the room at the Land Shark Lager and Red Stipe neon beer signs. He gazed at the vintage surfing pictures and the autographed photo of Key West's favorite son, Ernest Hemingway. He looked at the tattered and faded *Key Largo* and *Endless Summer* movie posters. He glanced up at the long boards that hung from the ceiling, praying, as he always did, that Red had secured them properly. Jimmy Buffett's "Come Monday" was playing on the juke box. His flip-flops peeled away from the sticky floor with an audible slurp as he climbed aboard his favorite orange stool and rested his forearms on the bar. Dan felt as though he was seeing an old friend for the first time in a long time.

"I really missed this place," he said just barely above a whisper.

"What's that?" Red asked.

"Nothing," Dan replied.

Red scanned the room. "Where's Mel?"

"Shit." Dan looked around to see Mel fumbling with his fly as he exited the men's room. "Everything okay, Mel?" he called out.

"Had to pee," Mel called back from across the room. A few heads turned and Dan and Red chuckled. Mel climbed aboard his own stool. "Do you have a wine list?"

"Sure do," Red answered, sliding a small cardboard teepee from its resting place, next to the napkin holder, over in front of Mel.

Mel picked it up and studied it.

"Tequila, Seven, and lime for me, Red." The words rolled off Dan's tongue for the millionth time.

Red grabbed the tequila bottle and sat it on the bar. He grabbed a glass, filled it with ice and poured a shot into the glass. Grabbing the soda gun he filled the glass the rest of the way with 7UP. He flipped open the lid of the plastic tray containing the fruit, dropped a lime into Dan's glass, and pushed it across the bar to his friend, leaving a trail of condensation behind.

Dan pulled the lime from the drink, gave it a squeeze, and dropped it back in. He wrapped his hand around the glass, raised it to his lips, and took a big drink. "Ahh," he said as he felt the cold liquid wash over his tongue, down his throat, and into his belly. The first drink after a long time with no drink is always the best drink. Dan swore he could feel the tequila spread to his veins and then to his arms, his legs, and throughout his whole body. It felt good. *Damn* good. He loved drinking more than he knew he should, and even felt a little guilty. He took another sip.

"Decide what you want there, Trap … or should I call you Mel?" Red asked.

"I would have preferred you call me Mel but I think I'm starting to like the nick name, Trap."

"Just call him Mel," Dan chimed in.

"Then Mel it is," Mel said, pointing his finger in the air. "And I will have a grape soda, sir!"

"We don't have grape."

Mel shot his finger into the air once again. "I will have an orange soda!"

Red shook his head no.

And again Mel's finger went skyward. "What kind of soda do you have?"

"Coke, Diet Coke, 7UP, ginger-ale," Red listed as he held the soda gun paused in mid-air.

"I will have water!"

Chapter Twenty

It was a few minutes after midnight when Red dropped Mel and Dan at the front door of 632 Beach View Street. Mel climbed from the front seat and pulled the seat forward for Dan. The two men said good night to Red and Mel followed Dan up the gravel pathway to the front door. The old screen door squeaked as Dan pulled it open. Dan pulled back the welcome mat to retrieve the key, unlocked the door, and pushed it open.

Mel looked down and read the welcome mat as he stepped over it, THE COAST'S. "Do you live with your parents?" Mel asked.

"Good God, no," Dan answered.

"Wife?"

"No"

"Who's the other Coast then?" Mel asked, looking around the living room.

"My wife's dog."

Dan went directly to the bar that sat against the far wall of the dining room.

"Where is she?"

Mel sat in Dan's La-Z-Boy.

"She's a he," Dan replied. Someone had removed every bottle of alcohol from the bar. *Sonofabitch*, he thought.

"Your wife was a he?" Mel picked up the remote control from the end table and turned on the television.

"The dog is a he; my wife was a she." Dan went to the kitchen and opened the cupboard door above the sink. It was bare *Goddammit, Mom.*

"And now your wife is a he? Did she have one of those operations or something?" Mel surfed through the channels finally coming to rest on an old episode of *Dragnet*.

Dan slammed the cupboard door. "Mel, do you think you could shut the fuck up for a few minutes?"

"Sure thing," Mel answered, setting the remote back down and reclining back in the chair.

Dan passed back through the dining room on his way to his bedroom. "Thank you." He opened his closet. The top shelf sat empty. *Shit. You're nothing if not thorough, Mom.*

"You looking for something?" Mel asked when Dan returned to the living room.

"No."

"You want to watch *Dragnet* with me?"

"Thanks, but I think I'm gonna hit the hay."

"Are ya sure? It's a good show; it reminds me of when I used to work bunco out in L.A."

"I'd like to hear about that sometime, Mel, but I'm tired." Dan turned and went back down the hall to his bedroom.

"Oh, come on," Mel insisted. He called out in a deep baritone: "Dum-de-DUM-DUM! Dum-de-dum-dum-DUMMMM!

"You sure are," Dan muttered wearily as he shut his door.

Chapter Twenty-One

Dan rolled onto his back and stared up at the ceiling through the motionless ceiling fan, the sun beamed through the bedroom window. He stretched his arms upward and then tucked them in under is head. He was glad to be waking up in his own bed.

A dog barked and he thought of Buddy, his own dog. Then it was quiet except for the sound of the television. Dan lay still trying to place the familiar voice coming from the idiot box. *Fess Parker*, he thought, *Daniel Boone*. He rolled over and looked at the clock. 10:23.

Dan threw back his covers, swung his legs over the edge of the bed, and pulled on the same shorts he had worn the day before. He went to his dresser and grabbed a T-shirt; a concert T__, The Fixx, *Phantoms Tour*, 1984. *Great album. Great concert*, he thought.

In the hall, Dan pushed open the guest room door. Mel was not in his bed. *Early riser*.

Or so it seemed. Mel was sound asleep in the La-Z-Boy.

Dan went to the kitchen to make coffee.

"Mel," Dan called from the kitchen.

Mel stirred in the recliner.

"Hey."

Mel opened his eyes. "Where am I?"

Dan stood in the doorway between the dining room and the kitchen. "My house."

Mel sat up straight and looked around the room. "Oh, yeah."

"Did you go bed last night?" Dan asked.

"Bed? You didn't tell me to go to bed."

"I didn't think I *had* to tell you to go to bed."

"You didn't even tell me I had a bed here."

Dan forced an uncomfortable smile. "Jeez, sorry, Mel. There's a bedroom at the end of the hall, the door on the left. You can sleep in there tonight."

"Thanks, Dan, that's really nice of you."

"Um, yeah, don't mention it." Dan returned to the coffee pot. "Mel, you want a cup of coffee?"

"I don't think I'm supposed to have caffeine. It makes me crazy."

Yeah, that's what makes you crazy. Dan opened the fridge. "We're gonna have to go out for breakfast, there's nothing here in the fridge."

"Can I have a glass of water?"

"Sure, Mel." Dan poured himself a cup of coffee and then a glass of water for his guest. Then he went to the porch to grab the morning paper. On his way back through the living room he said, "I usually have coffee in the back yard. How's that sound?"

"I'm not supposed to have caffeine."

"I know, but you can have your water while I have my coffee."

Mel got up quickly from his chair. "That sounds great. I like being outdoors."

"Me, too, Mel."

The two men walked out the kitchen door, down the steps, and along the gravel pathway that led to the two Adirondack chairs next to the fire pit. Another beautiful day in paradise.

Mel sat first and surveyed the yard. He looked out past the two palm trees that supported Dan's hammock at the beach.

"Nice place you have here, Dan," Mel commented. "I'd like to move down here and get myself a little place like this after I retire from the force."

Dan looked over the top of his newspaper. "Move down here?" he asked. "Where are you *originally* from?"

Mel took a sip of his water as he gazed out over the ocean. "Mockingbird Heights."

Dan slowly shook his head and lifted his paper.

The slam of a screen door diverted Mel's attention away from the island scenery. His head turned toward the house next door, and the woman standing on the back deck, palms resting on top of the wooden railing. It was Bev, Dan's neighbor, and friend. She was dressed in white denim shorts, cut just above the knee, and a blue and white striped tank top. Her blond hair was pulled back in a short ponytail__, an unusual hairdo for Bev__, and her feet were bare. Bev was in her late fifties but in Dan's opinion looked better—and sexier—than most women fifteen years her junior. Dan sometimes marveled that there had never been any romantic sparks between him and Bev. But she was no desperate cougar, and he had far too much respect for her to louse up the good thing they had with sex. So, they maintained the status quo.

"Wow," Mel whispered.

"I see they let you out of the hoosegow," Bev called out.

Dan grinned but kept his eyes on his reading material. "It was a nuthouse, madam, and you might say I sprung myself.

Bev was halfway across the yard, unintentionally doing her best walking-through-a-mine-field imitation, as she scouted for sharp objects in what Dan referred to as a lawn. "Sprung yourself, huh?" she said. "I bet there's a good story in there somewhere."

Mel rose quickly from his chair. "You can have my seat, miss."

Bev arched one shapely eyebrow. "Miss? Been awhile since I was a miss." She extended her hand. "You can call me Bev."

Mel gazed into her eyes and took her hand in both of his. "It's a pleasure to meet you, beautiful Bev. The name is Gormin, Mel Gormin. Please, take my chair."

Bev did as Mel so gallantly asked. "Why, thank you." She shot Dan a surprised grin; she liked being treated like a lady.

Dan pointed toward the small shed at the edge of the lawn. "There's a folding chair leaning against the woodshed over there, Mel."

Mel went to the shed, unfolded the chair, and seated himself.

"Uh, Mel, you can sit with us, if you like," Dan called out. He whispered to Bev, "He's kind of like Hymie the Robot from Get Smart. Takes everything literally."

"He's a little odd, all right. But cute as hell. And you could stand for some of his chivalry to rub off on you."

Mel gathered up his chair, placed it next to Bev, and sat down. "Can I get you a glass of water, Bev, or perhaps a nice hot cup of coffee?"

"Coffee would be wonderful, Mel. And a little sugar, please."

Mel stood. "There'll be time for a little sugar after we have become better acquainted, my dear." He winked and went toward the back door.

Bev watched Mel as he trudged up the gravel path to the backdoor. "A real charmer."

"Yeah, Bev, about that__, I sprung him out of the nuthouse, too."

"I knew it! What did *he* do?"

"He didn't do anything."

"Why was he in the nuthouse?"

"Because he's nuts."

Bev deflated and slumped in her chair. "Figures. All the good ones are either crazy or gay." Bev thought for a moment. "How crazy?"

Dan once again peered over the top of his newspaper. "What?"

"I mean is he a little bit *eccentric* crazy or is he full-blown *here's Johnny* crazy?"

"He's somewhere in between, I think. Why?"

"Oh I don't know. He is handsome."

Mel returned with the coffee. "Here you are my lady."

"Thank you, Mel." Bev batted her eyelashes.

Only in Key West, Dan thought.

After Dan and Bev had finished their second cup of coffee, and Mel had entertained Bev with tales of his days as a homicide detective in Mockingbird Heights, complete with shootouts that had perps *going ahead and making his day* and wild car chases in his red and white 1974, Ford Torino, Dan was exhausted. Mel's pop culture-informed delusions jumped from *The Munsters* to *Sudden Impact* to *Starsky and Hutch* in a gleeful routine worthy of the late, great Robin Williams. Now Dan knew why liked Mel so much: He was a bona fide bat shit-crazy version of his TV and movie obsessed self.

Laying the newspaper in his lap Dan said, "Come on, Mel, we better get in the house and come up with a game plan."

Mel stood and turned to Bev. "Bev, it was an immense pleasure to meet you. I look forward to spending more time with you while I am in town."

Bev gave her hand to Mel, and he kissed it. "Maybe you and Dan can come over for dinner this evening," she said with a hopeful gleam in her eye.

"That would be wonderful. Until then, my lady."

Dan rolled his eyes. "Come on, lover boy."

Chapter Twenty-Two

Dan and Mel stood in Dan's front yard. "Where's your car?" Mel asked.

"Long story," Dan replied. He glanced across the street and saw Edna McGee's front curtain pull back. Dan couldn't see her but he knew she was watching, keeping tabs on the neighborhood. Beach View Street's own one woman neighborhood watch. Dan waved. "Good morning, Mrs. McGee," he hollered across the street. The curtain dropped back into place.

Mel backed up and sat on the steps. "Are we going to walk to my sister's house?"

"No." Dan looked over toward the mini-van sitting in Bev's driveway, he wondered if he should ask to borrow it.

"Should we ask Bev for a ride?"

"No." Dan pulled his cell phone from the front pocket of his cargo shorts.

"Should we call Red for a ride?"

"Mel, can you shut up for a second?" Dan tapped the front of his cell a few times and put it to his ear. "Hey, I need a ride somewhere. Does it matter where? Okay." Dan hung up the phone.

Edna McGee's front door opened. She opened the lid to her mailbox and let it drop. She knew the mail didn't come until three. She looked across the street at Dan and then did a double take. "Oh, Dan," she called out. "I didn't know you were home." She threw a finger in the air. "Wait right there for a second.

"I'm not going anywhere," he yelled back.

A few seconds later Edna was on her way across the street, carrying a paper plate. She was dressed in her usual uniform; an old lady house dress like the one Norman Bates' stuffed mother wore and black sneakers. Her hair, which she had recently cut a little shorter and let go gray, was sitting in a small, tight bun on top of her head. She smiled as she neared.

"I baked you some cookies this morning, Dan. I know you didn't get to eat any of the ones I baked you for Christmas, what with …you know, the trouble and all."

Dan took the plate. "Thanks, Edna. That was very nice of you."

Edna peered around Dan at the unfamiliar man on the steps. "Who's your friend?"

Mel stood, approached, and held out his hand.

"Edna this is Mel, Mel this is Edna."

Edna held out her hand and Mel seized it warmly in both of his. "It's a pleasure to meet you, exquisite Edna. The name is Gormin, Mel Gormin."

Dan shook his head. *Oh, for Chrissakes, did he swallow a goddamn thesaurus?*

Edna smiled, revealing a set of dentures in need of a good Efferdent soak. "It's nice to meet you."

"Would you like to come in for a cup of coffee and let us sample some of the marvelous cookies you've baked?" Mel suggested.

Dan said, "Red's on his way to pick us up, Mel."

"Don't be rude, Dan," Mel chastised him.

Edna declined the offer. "Thank you, but I really have to get back in the house and finish my laundry."

"Maybe next time," Mel offered.

Edna returned to her house and gave one last wave before going in.

"Wonderful woman," Mel said.

"Exquisite," Dan replied, matter-of-factly.

Red's car skidded to a stop. *Thank God.*

"Shotgun!" Mel shouted.

"Dammit!"

Red took a right onto Atlantic Boulevard and then a left on George Street. "Say there, Danno, where are we going?" he asked.

"Ask Mel," Dan replied. "This is his caper."

Mel wasn't paying attention. He was leaning forward, looking up in the sky.

"Mel," Dan said.

Mel rolled down the window and stuck his head out.

Dan tapped him on the shoulder. "Mel!"

"What?"

"Where does your sister live?"

"My sister?"

"Yeah. Where does she live?"

Mel turned and looked at Dan, muttered, "I have no idea," and stuck his head back out the window. From Dan's point of view, there wasn't much difference between Mel and his mutt Buddy when he took the latter for a car ride. Mel had the same joyful, innocent look on his face. And slobbered almost as much.

Red looked at Dan in the rearview mirror. Dan shrugged. "Mel!"

Mel rolled up the window. "I think we're being followed."

Dan turned around and looked out the back window.

Mel pointed his finger in the air. "Not back there, up there," he said. "Sometimes I can see satellites, you know, taking pictures. There's one right above us even as we speak, and it's been following us since we left your house."

Red gave Mel a confused look and scooted closer to his door.

"Shit!" Dan said.

"What?" Red asked.

"Turn around and go back to my house."

"Did you forget something?"

"Yeah, Mel's medication. Satellites."

*****

Once Mel was medicated and the three were back on the road, Dan asked, "Mel, you really don't know your sister's address?"

"No. I've never even been to her house. We lived in an apartment when we first got here and she bought the house after I went in the hospital. I've seen pictures; maybe we could just drive around until I see it."

"Yeah, great idea," Dan said sarcastically, then pulled his phone from his pocket and dialed.

A woman's voice came from the other end. "Lower Keys Medical Center. How may I direct your call?"

"I need to speak to a nurse there … Maxine Myers."

"May I ask who's calling?"

"Yes. Tell her it's Dr. Mark Sloan," Dan answered.

"Please hold."

"Hello, Maxine Myers speaking."

"Maxine, its Dan. I need an address for Mel's sister."

Maxine paused for a moment. "I'm fine, how are you?"

Dan sighed. "How are you, Maxine?"

"I'm good. How are you?"

Bite your lip, Danny boy. Play nice. Go through the motions. "I'm good. I was wondering if you could do me a big favor, please."

"Sure, Dan. What is it?"

"I need an address for Mel's sister."

"Sure, hold on for a second."

Dan waited as he stared into the rearview mirror at a grinning Red. He flipped him the bird.

"Here it is," Maxine said. "Stacey Gormin, 1004 Catherine Street, second house from the corner."

"Is there a contact number?"

"Um, no, that's weird."

"Okay thanks." Dan lowered his voice. "Hey, um …can I call you later?"

"Why?"

"I thought maybe, ya know … we could go out sometime."

"Sure, that would be nice."

"Okay then, talk to you later."

Dan hung up the phone and returned it to his pocket.

"Danny's got a girlfriend," Red sang.

"How about you drink a nice big cup of shut the Christ up?" Dan seethed.

Mel joined in singing, "Danny's got a girlfriend, Danny's got a girlfriend."

"Red, you bastard, see what you started?"

Mel's homely voice soared. "Danny and Maxine, sitting in a tree, k-i-s-s-i-n-g! First comes love, then comes marriage—"

"Shut up!"

"—then comes baby in a baby carriage."

Dan flashed back to his closet quickie with Maxine. Had she used protection? Dear God, I hope so."

Chapter Twenty-Three

Red slowed to a halt at the stop sign on the corner of Flagler and Reynolds. A white dump truck with BARRACUDA BUILDERS on the door was parked on Reynolds Street. Orange safety cones circled the truck. A white van, with the same lettering, sat in the parking lot on the corner of Reynolds and Seminole. Three men in hard hats were repairing the block wall that surrounded the parking lot.

Red looked in his rearview mirror at Dan. "Pretty hot out there today," Red mentioned. "You might want to think about bringing those guys a case of Land Shark for after work."

Dan watched as one of the men removed his hard hat and wiped his brow with the back of his hand. "I'm probably paying them today. You know, since I'm the one who crashed my car through it." he said. "But you're probably right, I guess I should."

Red swung the Firebird around the corner onto Reynolds, up a few blocks and a right onto United, a quick left at Grinnel Street, and finally a left on Catherine Street, where he pulled to the edge of the blacktop. The Firebird's tires crunched the crushed stone.

The trio exited the car. Dan surveyed the property and gave the house a once-over. A new gray Toyota Corolla sat in the driveway, facing the street.

"Nice place," Dan commented. "What's your sister do for a living?"

Mel walked up the brick pathway and through the white picket fence toward the front door. "She paints a little," he answered. "She's really good."

Dan followed Mel up the walkway. "Seems like the rent on this place would be a little high for someone who, *paints a little*," Dan observed.

"She doesn't rent, she owns this house. I help her out with the mortgage."

Dan glanced at Red with a grin. "I bet you do, officer."

Mel knocked on the door.

Red walked around the fence and into the driveway. The passenger side window was down. He looked inside. "The keys are in the ignition," he said.

Mel knocked again.

Red went to the rear of the Toyota. "The trunk is popped."

Mel knocked once more.

Red pulled the trunk open with the tips of his fingers.

Mel lifted his fist to knock.

"Mel, she's not here," Dan said and went to join Red at the rear of the vehicle.

Mel left the porch and walked around the house to the back yard.

"Someone was going on a trip," Red deduced. In the trunk were two small suitcases and a matching bag.

"Looks that way," Dan agreed.

Mel walked up between Dan and Red. "She doesn't answer the back door either," he said. "Maybe she went to the beach."

Dan stepped aside to give Mel a look at the suitcases. "I don't think so, Mel. It looks like she had planned on going away for a while."

Mel reached inside his shirt and pulled out his badge. "We'd better canvas the area and talk with her neighbors, find out when she was last seen." Mel pointed to the house next door. "Red, you start with that house, and I'll hit the other neighbor. Dan, you see if you can gain entrance through the back door."

Dan was surprised. "Good idea, Mel, but let's put the badge away. Just tell them you're her brother. They would probably rather talk to a family member than a cop anyway."

Mel nodded. "Good thinking!"

The three men separated.

Dan was halfway around the house when he decided it was best not to leave Mel alone. He quickly spun around and joined him on the porch of the house next door.

Mel knocked and then pressed the doorbell. He started to knock again.

"Give it a second, for Chrissakes," Dan mumbled.

Mel dropped his arm back at his side and loudly sighed.

As they waited for an answer Dan glanced over to see Red talking with a man in the front yard, two houses down.

Mel knocked again.

"Just a minute," came a voice from inside the house and a few seconds later the door creaked open. An elderly gentleman in a white wife-beater and red striped boxer shorts looked Mel and Dan up and down with undisguised distaste and distrust. Before Dan could speak the man raised his hand to shush him. "I don't want to buy anything, I don't want to sell anything, I'm already on a first-name basis with my Lord and savior, and you can take your reverse mortgage and shove it up your ass."

"I'm looking for my sister," Mel blurted out.

The old man tapped the front of his boxers crudely. "Don't know your sister, and haven't had a use for any woman since '92, if ya know what I mean."

"No, sir, I don't know what you mean," Mel responded.

The old man shook his head, his cantankerousness blunted somewhat by Mel's absence of guile. "Is there something I can do for you boys?"

"We're looking for the woman who lives next door, Stacey Gormin." Dan pointed at Mel. "This is her brother, Mel Gormin. He hasn't seen or heard from her in the past few weeks and he's starting to get a little worried. We just thought we would check with a few of her neighbors and see if they had seen or heard anything from her."

The old man scratched the gray stubble on his chin and looked Mel over once again. "You're her brother, ya say?"

"Yes, sir." Mel nodded.

Ship of Fools

Mel and Dan backed up as the old man tottered out on to the porch.

"Nice girl, that Stacey," the old man said as he looked over at her car in the driveway. "Painted me a picture a few years back__, a picture of me and Buster, my dog. Buster got hit by a car right out front, here; the bastard just drove off and left him to die in the street. A few days later Stacey came over with the painting. Yeah, she's a real nice girl." The old man's eyes began to well. "I sure miss that dog."

"I'm sorry for your loss, sir," said Mel with genuine compassion. "Have you seen Stacey lately?"

The old man thought for a second. "Nope. As a matter of fact, I guess I haven't seen her in a couple of weeks."

"Have you noticed anything strange going on over there in the last few weeks?" Dan asked.

"Strange?" the man asked. "What do you mean by strange?"

"I don't know," Dan answered. "Anything that made you think, *hey,* that's strange."

"Don't be a smartass, young man. No, not that I can think of."

"Well, thanks for your time, sir," Mel said. "If you think of anything else you can give my partner a call."

Dan reached into his front pocket, pulled out one of his business cards, and handed it to the man. "My cell phone number is on the card."

"Dan Coast," the old man read aloud. "Hey, you're that private eye guy that went crazy and drove your car into a brick wall on Christmas morning. Read all about you in the paper."

"Yeah, that's me," Dan responded.

"Locked him up in the nut house," Mel added.

"*Really?*" Dan seethed as he turned and left the porch.

"Yeah, the only way they would let him out of the loony bin was in my custody," Mel said. "Now, together we solve crimes. Right now we're landlubbers, but as soon as headquarters okays the funds, we'll be hitting the high seas. So watch out, all you pirates and drug smugglers!"

The old man laughed until he was bent over wheezing. "Sounds like one of those old detective shows," he said when he had composed himself. "You could call the show, *"Ship of Fools."*

Mel thought for a second. "I like it."

"Come on, Mel," Dan called out.

"See you later, sir," Mel said as he rejoined Red and Dan in front of Stacey's house.

"Neighbor hasn't seen her in a few weeks," Red said.

"Yeah, that guy either," Dan said and motioned for Red to follow.

Dan, Red, and Mel combed all sides of the house. Red tried to look in each window as he passed but all the shades were closed. Mel looked over and saw the old man next door watching them from a side window. Mel waved. The man waved back and left the window.

Dan tried the back door, it was locked. He pressed his forehead up against the glass and shaded his eyes from the sun. He was looking into the kitchen. "We're gonna have to break the glass and let ourselves in, Mel."

Red bent and pulled back the matt. "Let's use this key instead."

Dan said, "Good idea."

Red unlocked the door and Dan eased it open. Mel pushed by and went in first. "Stacey!" he called out. "Stacey, its Mel! Are you home?"

"Dirty dishes in the sink," Red commented. "And there's a cup here with a tea bag in it."

Dan walked into the living room. "The TV is on." He picked up the remote off of the coffee table and turned it off.

Mel was upstairs and had yelled Stacey's name a few more times. He walked back down the stairs. "She's nowhere."

"She's somewhere," Dan said.

Red went up the stairs and patted Mel on the shoulder as he walked by. "Don't worry," said Red optimistically, we'll find her, pal."

Chapter Twenty-Four

After the three amateur sleuths had finished up their investigation at Stacey Gormin's residence, and found nothing__, other than the two packed suitcases, the television being on, and the tea cup, that any of them would consider a clue, they went to Red's for lunch.

Dan sat at his usual stool with Mel to his left. Red slid a tequila, Seven, and lime across the bar to Dan and then made himself a Scotch and ginger.

"May I see the wine list?" Mel asked.

"Water it is," Red answered.

Mel opened a menu and scanned the items. "What type of burger would you recommend, Red?"

"Ham."

"Ham-burger." Mel cocked his head in thought. "That sounds good; I think I'll have one of those... with fries, please."

"Coming right up. What do you want, Dan?"

"Fish sandwich and fries."

Red jotted their order on a guest check and walked the four steps to the kitchen door. "Order up, Jocko."

Jocko, the longtime cook at Red's Bar and Grill, grunted and pulled the cigar from his mouth, laid it on the edge of the stove, wiped his nose with the back of his hand, grabbed the ticket, and jammed it into a clothespin that hung from a thin wire above his head.

"Everything okay, Jocko?" Red asked.

Jocko dismissed Red with the wave of his hand and grunted once again.

Red said, "Okay," stepped back and let the door swing shut.

When Red returned Dan's empty glass sat at the edge of the bar. Red refilled it and slid it back.

Dan squeezed the lime juice into his glass and dropped the lime back in the drink. "I gotta get me a car," he said.

Mel sipped his water. "You can use my car if you want to, Dan"

"You have a nice car do ya, Mel?" Red asked.

"Yes, it's in storage."

"Let me guess," Dan smirked. "Is it a red McLaren that says coyote down the side of it?"

Mel laughed. "No, Dan, you're thinking of the car from *Hardcastle and McCormick*. My car is a red Ferrari, kind of like Magnum's, but newer."

"Of course it is," Dan grumbled and went back to his drink.

Red laughed out loud. "You'll have to take me for a ride in in that Ferrari sometime, Mel."

"Sure thing, Red," Mel agreed. "But like I said, it's in storage right now."

Dan wanted to scream. "Back to reality, what are ya gonna do with Jimmy P.'s Volkswagen Bug out there, Red?" he said, referencing a gangster from an earlier escapade.

"I was gonna put a for sale sign on her, I just haven't gotten around to it yet. You can use it till ya get yourself another car if ya want."

"I will, thanks."

Red turned and grabbed a set of car keys hanging from a nail over the back bar and tossed them in front of Dan. "It's all yours, but remember, no drinking and driving__, that's *my* insurance."

Dan frowned. "It's like you've never met me."

Chapter Twenty-Five

Dan slid his empty plate across the bar and got up from his stool. "You about done there, Mel?"

Mel stuffed the last few French fries into his face and stood. "Yes."

Dan patted his front pockets. "I'll have to get you next time, Red, left my wallet at home."

Red picked up the empty plates. "Yeah, I'll put it on your tab," he grumbled. "Ya know, you would think someone with your kind of money, Mr. Doesn't-Have-To-Hold-Down-A-Real-Job-Because-I-Won-The-Frickin'-Lottery, would carry a little of it with him."

"Well, sorry, I don't really have access to it at this time," Mel said matter-of-factly.

"I think he was talking to me, Mel," Dan said.

"Oh. Did you really win the frickin' lottery?"

"I did indeed."

"Cool," Mel beamed. "Then we can pool our finances and start patrolling the high seas on our TV show."

"Ship of Fools, right?"

Mel's finger shot skyward. "Check! I shall be the captain. You shall be the first mate." Predictably, he began whistling the Gilligan's Island theme tunelessly.

"Swell," Dan sighed.

The two men were making their way across the parking lot toward the pink Volkswagen Bug as a familiar car came to a stop next to them. It was Cindy Leonard, the bartender at Red's Bar and Grill. Dan smiled big. The door opened and Cindy climbed out. Her long blond hair was pulled back in a ponytail, like most days, and she was wearing white capris, an orange tank-top and white deck shoes.

"Hey, stranger," Dan said, "I didn't think you were ever coming back."

Cindy was twenty-three. She was originally from Highland Park, a suburb of Chicago. But after falling in love with Key West during a spring break a few years back she dropped out of college and decided to stay. Not having children of his own, Dan didn't know what it felt like to have a daughter, but he imagined that the feelings were probably similar to the way he felt about Cindy.

"Cindy threw her arms around Dan and squeezed him tight. "Miss me, did you?"

"Not really," he joked. "I just don't trust anyone else to bring in my mail and watch my dog."

Cindy giggled. "About that … when do you want Buddy back?"

"I don't."

"We can't keep him forever."

"What time do you get off work?"

"Not till two, but I can call Derrick and have him bring him by your place. He gets out of work at three today."

"Sounds good. If I'm not there the key is under the mat. Just tell him to let Buddy in."

Mel sighed loudly.

"Spring a leak?" Dan asked him.

"Who's your friend?" Cindy asked.

Dan stepped aside in anticipation of the usual introduction ritual. Mel stuck out his hand. "The names Gormin, Mel Gormin. It's a pleasure to meet you, miss. And you are?"

Cindy took his hand and shook. "Leonard, Cindy Leonard."

Mel took his left hand and put it on top of Cindy's. "Ah, sexy Cindy," he said and winked.

Dan grabbed Cindy's arm and yanked it away from Mel. "Okay, that's enough, let's go."

Cindy laughed and walked up the steps and into Red's as Dan and Mel resumed their walk to the Bug.

"Beautiful girl," Mel commented. "Is she married?"

Dan opened the door to the Volkswagen and climbed in. "No, but she has a boyfriend."

Mel got in. "Are they exclusive?"

"Yes, Mel, but that doesn't matter because you're twice her age *and* you live in the nut house."

Mel slammed his door. "Ouch! That was a bit abrasive."

112

Dan started the engine and pulled out of the parking lot.

Mel inspected the interior of the car and then fastened his seatbelt. "Pretty nice car, I guess, but nowhere near as nice as my Ferrari."

"Shut up, Mel."

Mel rolled down his window and looked up at the sky.

"Looking for satellites?" Dan asked.

"Don't be stupid, Dan, they turn on their cloaking devices in the afternoon."

"Oh yeah, what was I thinking?"

Chapter Twenty-Six

Dan sat in his Adirondack chair next to the fire pit. He had built a small fire and was sipping a tequila, Seven, and lime. The morning's newspaper lay on the ground next to his chair. He pulled his cell phone from his pocket, stared at it for a few seconds, and then dropped it on the newspaper. He took another sip of his drink and thought about lying in his hammock.

A car door shut behind him, and he turned to see Bev standing next to her mini-van. He watched as she went to the rear of the van and opened the hatch. She grabbed a few bags of groceries, closed the hatch, and started down the driveway to the rear of her house. She waived and Dan held his drink in the air. He thought about helping her, but that would involve getting out of his chair.

Bev climbed the three steps that led to her deck and went through the back door. Dan turned back and looked at his phone once again, He picked it up and scrolled through his contacts until he came to Maxine's name.

Dan was nervous. He hadn't asked a woman out on a date since Candi, with an "i". A few one-night stands here and there don't really count as dates. He tapped the back button and then the contacts icon. He scrolled through until he came to Candi's name. *I wonder what Candi's up to?* he thought. *I wonder if she is seeing anyone.* He wondered if the new guy had *extra baggage*, if he drank *too much*, and was *too* immature.

Bev's back door slammed, and Dan looked over his shoulder. Bev was approaching with a glass of red wine in one hand and a light blue sweater in the other. She sat in the empty chair.

"Where's your friend?" she inquired.

"Taking a nap. The medication he gets in the afternoon knocks him right out."

Bev sipped her wine and Dan downed the rest of his drink.

"Any word on his sister?"

"Her neighbors haven't seen her in a few weeks."

"Where do you go from here?"

"There's an orderly, Lonnie, that works at the hospital that Mel and I had a little trouble with. I think he may know something about all of this. Probably head over to his house tonight and have a word with him. Kind of wanted Red to go with me though."

"Lonnie a scary dude?"

"Not scary, just big."

"You want another drink?" Bev asked.

Dan swirled the remaining ice as he inspected his glass. "Yeah, I'll make it."

"Wait," Bev said. "I have something I want you to try."

Dan scowled. "Do I have to?"

"Yes."

"Okay."

Bev sat her glass on the ground next to her and returned home. When Dan heard the door close he picked up his phone and tapped the screen a few times.

"Hello," Maxine answered.

"Hi... It's Dan."

"I know."

"What's up?"

"Nothing."

"So... you, uh... wanna do something tomorrow night?"

"Like what?"

"I dunno, have a drink, see a movie."

"Okay."

"Okay."

"What time?"

"I get out of work at four. So... Six?"

"Okay."

"Then I'll pick you up at six."

"Okay."

"Bye."

"Bye."

Dan was still grinning as Bev returned with his glass. "What are you grinning about?"

"Nothing."

Bev handed him his drink. "It must be something. You're grinning like the village idiot."

"Which I am, I'm told. On the plus side, I have a date tomorrow night at six."

Bev nodded her head toward Dan's house. "That's great, but what are you going to do with your house guest, bring him with you?"

"Christ, no!"

"Can he stay here by himself?"

Dan just stared at Bev with a devilish grin.

"Oh, no," Bev said, shaking her head. "I'm not watching him."

Dan continued to stare, widening his eyes and cocking his head just a bit.

"Fine, he can come over to my house ... but you better be home early."

Dan raised his hand in a close-enough Boy Scout salute. "I promise."

Dan's back door slammed shut. Dan and Bev looked over to see Mel yawning and stretching his arms above his head. "Glorious night," he called out.

"Glorious," Dan repeated.

Mel walked to the woodshed and grabbed a folding chair and placed it next to Bev. "How are you this evening, beautiful Bev?"

"Glorious, Mel, just glorious," she answered.

At that moment Derrick and Buddy rounded the corner of the house. Dan stood and Buddy started running. Dan couldn't help but smile as he walked toward his dog. Buddy ran around him and went right to Bev, his tail wagging a mile a minute.

"Looks like he missed someone," Derrick said.

"Yeah... someone," Dan said as he sat back down. "Can I get you a drink, Derrick?"

"No, thanks, I'm going to head over to Red's and have dinner with Cindy."

"How was your trip to Chicago?" Bev asked.

"Let's just say I'm glad to be home."

Dan pointed at Mel. "Derrick this is Mel; Mel, Derrick."

Mel gave a slight wave. "Nice to meet you, Derrick."

Dan did a double take at Mel. "Can't think of anything that starts with D? Devine Derrick, delightful Derrick, dazzling Derrick. Nothing?"

"Don't be ridiculous, Dan, Derrick is a man. Wouldn't I sound a little crazy introducing myself to a man in that manner?"

Dan rolled his eyes. "Yeah, Mel, what was I thinking? We wouldn't want you to sound crazy."

Derrick was confused. "Okay, then, talk to you guys later. It was nice meeting you, Mel."

"I need another drink," Dan said. "What was in that drink, Bev? It tasted different."

She smiled. "You liked that?"

"Yes, I did. I didn't think you could improve on tequila, Seven, and lime."

"It was the ice cubes, they were coconut water. Wendy, a friend of mine from Maine, was in town a few weeks ago. She gave me the idea."

Dan held out his glass. "More, please."

"Wonderful Wendy," Mel whispered to himself.

Bev climbed out of her chair, took Dan's glass and her own. "Would you like something to drink, Mel?"

"Yes, thank you, Bev. What type of wine is that you are drinking?"

"It's a Merlot."

"Hmm, Merlot sounds good. I think I'll have a glass of water, please, on the rocks if it wouldn't be too much trouble."

"Coming right up," Bev said and went back to her house with Buddy following close behind.

Dan said to Mel. "Hey, Mel, I have a date tomorrow night and I was wondering if you would like to hang out over at Bev's for the evening."

"That would be great, Dan. It would give Bev and I a chance to get better acquainted. I'll need to shave and get a haircut. Maybe we could even get to the store tomorrow so I could pick up a new shirt."

"Mel, it's not a date."

"You said it was a date."

"Mine is a date."

"Then why can't mine be a date?"

"Because you and Bev are just friends, that's why. You're just gonna hang out, maybe watch TV or something."

Mel looked disappointed. "That's fine I guess. One can never have too many friends, I guess."

"Exactly."

Mel stared out over the beach and the water; he was far away. "I had a wife once."

"What did you say?"

Mel didn't answer.

"Mel," Dan said.

Mel blinked and shook his head. "What?" he asked.

"What did you say, Mel?"

"Nothing."

Bev returned with Mel's ice water and fresh drinks for her and Dan.

"Dan's going on a date tomorrow night Bev. Is it okay if I come over to your house and hang out with you, just as friends, and watch a movie or something?"

"Sure, that would be great, Mel."

Mel turned his attention to Dan. "Dan who are you going on a date with?"

"A woman I met."

"How long have you known her?"

"A few weeks."

"Are you going on a date with Maxine, Dan?"

Dan sighed. "Yes, Mel."

"I figured."

"Who is Maxine?" Bev asked.

"She's a nurse at the hospital," Mel explained. "Her and Dan had sex in the janitors closet."

Dan spit his drink through his nose. "How the hell did you know about that?"

"Harry Marry told me."

"How the hell did she know?"

"Billy Maple told her."

"That's just great."

Bev couldn't stop laughing. "My God, Dan, you are one classy fella."

Chapter Twenty-Seven

Dan stood in the dining room, flipping through the white pages for Lonnie Rook's address. He squinted and then opened his eyes as wide as he could, trying his best to focus on the small, fuzzy black letters. He picked up the book and held it as far from his face as he could and slowly brought it back.

"Maybe you need glasses," Mel offered.

"Maybe you need a muzzle," Dan responded.

"How long has it been since you had your eyes checked?"

Dan dropped the book back on the table. "There's nothing wrong with my eyes, goddammit! The letters are too small, and when they print the book it looks blurry."

Mel moved up behind Dan and looked over his shoulder. "Looks okay to me."

"That's probably because *you* need glasses and everything else looks blurry to you, so this phone book looks normal."

"Huh, I never thought of it that way."

Dan slid the book to the side. "Here see if you can find Lonnie's address."

Mel ran his finger down the page. "Here it is, 828 Fleming Street."

Dan flipped the book closed. "Humph! Well, if you can read the ant-sized type in the phone book, you're defiantly gonna have to get your eyes checked."

"I guess *so*," Mel agreed. "I didn't realize how bad my eyes were. Thanks, Dan."

"Don't mention it. What are friends for?" Dan pulled out his cell phone and called Red. "Hey, you busy?"

"Why?"

"Because I want you to ride over to a guy's house with me."

"How big is he?"

"How did you know he was a big guy?"

"Because you never have me go with you to see a small guy."

"Can you go with me, or what?"

"It's really busy here and I had someone call in sick. Can't we go tomorrow?"

"Yeah, I guess that would be okay. What time's good for you?"

"Eleven?"

"Sounds good. I'll pick you up." Dan hung up his cell and tossed it on the phone book. "Looks like our plans have changed, Mel.

"We're not going over to talk to Lonnie?"

Dan made his way to the bar. "No, we'll skip that for tonight and go in the morning."

"Okay," Mel said and headed for the Lay-Z-Boy. "Yeah, I guess we can skip that."

Skip, Dan thought, as he stood in front of the fridge dropping ice cubes into his glass. *Skip*. Dan went back to the bar and poured a shot of tequila over the ice and then some 7UP.

Mel was flipping through the channels. "You want to watch *The King of Queens*?"

"I don't care." Dan picked up his cell phone.

"How about *Monk*?"

"I don't care, Mel."

"*I Killed My BFF*?"

"Jesus Christ, Mel, watch what you want." Dan dialed his phone and put it to his ear.

"*Forensic Files* it is."

Dan stood silently waiting, and suddenly Skip's voice came from the other end of the phone like Jeff Spicoli's long-lost brother. "Yo, dude... or dudette, whatever the case may be, you have reached Sir Skip Stoner. I am currently otherwise *occupato*. If you could please leave your name, number, breast size, and a short message, I will get back to you ... depending on the breast size ... unless you're a dude, then I'll just get back to you. Oh, yeah, bigger breasts, faster call-back. Over and out." There was a short pause and then: "Tiffany! How do I stop this thing from recording? What? Okay. *Beep.*"

"Skip, this is Dan Coast, give me a call back when you get this message, please." Dan tossed the phone back on the table. "Put it on *King of Queens*.

Chapter Twenty-Eight

Mel sat on the hardwood floor next to Buddy's bed. "This is a really nice dog, Dan," he commented. Both man and dog looked quite content.

Dan looked away from the TV. "Yeah, I guess."

"How long have you had him?"

"I don't know, five or six years, maybe."

Mel scratched Buddy between the ears. "He likes when you scratch his head."

"Yup."

"Where did you get him?"

Dan took a deep breath. The conversation was heading into a place Dan didn't want to go. "Cooperstown."

"Baseball Hall of Fame!" Mel exclaimed. "I always wanted to go there. We used to go to a lot of Dodgers games."

"We, who?" Dan asked.

Mel didn't answer. He just stared at the floor and ran his hand up and down Buddy's back. Buddy rolled over so Mel could scratch his belly.

"Is this your wife?" Mel asked, looking up at the photograph of Alex on the small table next to him.

Dan took another deep breath and his phone rang. He got up and went to the dining room table for his cell. "Hello."

"Dan the man! What's up, dude?" Skip asked. "Last I heard you was taking classes at the laughing academy."

"Laughing academy, that's a new one," Dan said.

"Hey, sorry, dude. Too soon? Ya know, dude, me and Tiff thought about coming to see you, but I figured you wouldn't want anyone gawking at you in that straightjacket, sucking your thumb and shit."

"I wasn't in a straitjacket, Skip."

"Were you sucking your thumb, dude? Cause if you were, that shit is safe with me, man."

"Skip, listen, I just need you to run over to a guy's house with me tonight so I can ask him a few questions."

"How big is he?"

"What the Christ? Can you go with me or not?"

"Sure, dude. I get out of work at six. I'll pick you up a few minutes after. I know you don't have a car any more, on account of you wrecked it when you flipped your gourd. It was in the paper."

"Yeah, we'll watch for ya a little after six." Dan hung up his phone and went to the bar to make a much needed drink.

"Who was that?"

"Skip. He's gonna take us over to Lonnie's."

Mel watched as Dan made his drink. "You sure drink a lot."

"No shit!"

"Do you drink alone?"

Dan turned and glared at Mel. "I wish!"

Mel took the hint and returned to rubbing Buddy's belly.

Chapter Twenty-Nine

It was 6:15. Dan stood in his driveway leaning against the pink Volkswagen Bug, Mel sat on the steps.

"Why can't we take him along?" Mel asked.

"Because I'm sure Skip doesn't want a dog riding in his car. Now give it a rest. Christ!"

Mel looked back at Buddy, who was sitting on the front porch looking forlornly out the screen door. "Sorry, Buddy, if it was up to me you could come with us, but someone else is a real hard ass."

Skip's bright yellow, 1974 Volkswagen Thing, top down, skidded to a stop in front of Dan's house. "Dan the man!" Skip shouted.

"Shotgun!" Mel shouted as he ran to the convertible.

Shit! Dan thought.

Skip looked at the pink Bug parked in the driveway. "Yo! Sweet ride, dude."

"Yeah," Dan responded as he climbed into the back seat. "A real sweet ride."

Mel held out his hand. "You must be Skip."

Skip shook Mel's hand. "Correctomundo! Skip Stoner at your service."

"Skip … Stoner," Dan echoed. "So, that's your real name?"

Skip laughed. "No. Who would name their kid Skip? My real name is Sean Stoner." He slammed the car into gear and they were off. "Where to?"

"828 Fleming Street," Mel blurted out.

"You got it," Skip said.

*****

Skip eased the car to the side of the street and parked. "828 Fleming Street," he announced. "Please make sure you have all of you belongings as you exit the vehicle." Skip shut off the engine and instead of opening his door, he jumped over it. Mel was impressed and did the same. Dan pulled the handle and let himself out.

"Can't jump over the door, Dan?" Mel asked.

"I'm sure I could have … if I wanted to."

"What's the guy's name we're looking for?" Skip asked.

"Lonnie Rook," Dan answered. His eyes focused on the windows in the second floor. "He must live in the apartment over this art gallery."

Ship of Fools

Mel read the closed sign on the gallery door. "Gallery's closed."

Dan tried the doorknob to the door that he assumed led upstairs to the apartment. "Door's locked."

Skip walked around the corner to the rear of the building. There was a small second story deck that came off the back.

Dan walked up beside Skip. "Anybody around?"

"Lonnie!" Skip shouted at the top of his lungs, startling Dan. "Lonnie Rook! We need to talk to you!"

"Jesus Christ!" Dan said. "What was that?"

"Didn't you want to talk to him?"

"Yeah," Dan responded, pointing around at a few onlookers. "But I didn't want everyone to know about it."

Skip shrugged. "Well, I don't think the dude's home any way. Step back!"

"What the Christ are ya gonna do?"

Skip placed his hands on the top rail of the fence and jumped. His feet landed on top of the fence, and then he leapt to the deck railing, pulling himself up and over and landing on the deck.

"Think you can do that, Dan?" Mel asked.

"Shut up, Mel."

"Go to the front, I'll let you guys in," Skip called down from the deck.

"I'll climb up like you, Skip," Mel hollered.

Dan grabbed Mel by the arm. "No, you won't."

When Dan and Mel arrived at the front door, Skip was already waiting. *"Entrez, s'il vous plait,"* he announced with a bow.

Dan went up the stairs and Mel and Skip followed.

At the top of the stairs Dan entered a small eat in kitchen. A tiny, white, wooden table was pushed against the wall, with two matching chairs placed neatly underneath the table. Beyond the kitchen was a living room about the same size with a sliding glass door that led to the deck. The kitchen and living room floors were light-colored linoleum, with a throw rug in the middle of the living room. All of the walls and moldings were white, and the apartment was very neatly kept.

Dan picked up a framed photograph from the coffee table. The photo was of Lonnie and an older woman who looked eerily similar to Lonnie. "Not what I expected Lonnie's apartment to look like," he commented, and replaced the picture.

Mel opened the bathroom door, walked in, and looked behind the shower curtain. "Clear!" he shouted.

Dan shook his head. *Clear.* He walked to the back door and out onto the deck. Nothing was out of place there either. He walked back in. "Not so much as a speck of dust or a spot on the carpet."

"There's a spot on the carpet in here," Skip called from the bedroom.

"What is it?" Dan asked, moving into the doorway.

"I think it's Lonnie's brains … and a lot of his blood."

Skip stepped aside to give Dan a better look. Sure enough, there was Lonnie, on the floor, next to the bed, face down in the carpet. What was left of the back of Lonnie's head looked like a half-eaten slice of watermelon.

Dan looked to his right at the blood and gray matter that had dried on its way down the wall. "That's gonna take a few coats of paint to cover."

Mel sidled up beside Dan. "Suicide?" he asked.

"Only if he hid the gun after he shot himself," Dan commented.

Mel looked at the floor. "Yeah, you're probably right. If he had hid the gun after he shot himself in the head there would be a trail of blood leading out of the room."

Skip looked confused. "Uh … yeah."

Mel turned and walked out of the room and back down the stairs.

Skip put his hand aside his mouth and whispered, "Yo, dude, I think that Mel guy is a few bricks short of a load."

"And it took you this long to notice. So what does that say about you, Skip?" Dan said, and followed Mel back down to the sidewalk.

"Ha! Dan the man, I never said *I* was normal."

When all three men were back at street level, they stood under the awning of the gallery. Mel turned to Dan and said, "You better call this one in, partner."

Dan went for his cell phone. "Yeah, I better. Rick's gonna love hearing from me."

Chapter Thirty

It was dark by the time Rick Carver came back down the stairs from Lonnie's apartment and joined Dan, Skip, and Mel on the sidewalk. Garish yellow crime scene tape was wrapped around each of the posts that supported the awning of the art gallery. Two patrol cars were parked in front of the gallery on Fleming Street and another sat on Margaret Street, their light bars flashing. Onlookers tried to get a peek and snapped pictures with their cameras and cell phones.

"The sliding glass door was open at the rear of the apartment," Rick said. "That must be how they gained entrance."

"I think I may have left the door ajar, dude," Skip commented.

Rick shook his head. "Some lattice on the deck was broken. Looks like they may have used the fence to jump up to the railing and kicked the lattice on their way over the railing."

Skip raised his hand. "Guilty."

Ship of Fools

Rick looked to Dan. "Goddammit, Coast, what made you think it was okay to trample all over a crime scene?"

"We didn't know it was a crime scene until it was too late. We just stopped over to have a talk with Lonnie Rook."

"Just stopped over," Rick questioned. "Do you always climb up the back of someone's house and break in when you want to have a few words with them?"

"Technically, we didn't break in constable—the door was unlocked," Skip offered.

"Shut up, Stoner! If I want any shit outta you I'll squeeze your goddamn head."

"Rick, I asked you to look into this guy but you just brushed it off. Maybe if you had come to see him he would still be alive." Dan knew he shouldn't have said it the second it left his mouth.

Rick pointed his finger at Dan. His hand shook, his lip quivered, and he spoke slowly through his teeth. "Listen, asshole, I don't take orders from you, and I sure as hell don't run around this island questioning people just because they kicked your ass. If anything, I should have looked him up and gave him a friggin' medal." Dan started to speak but Rick threw up a meaty paw to silence him. "Don't say a word, Coast, don't say a word. Now, you get yourself and these two morons out of my sight."

The three men headed for Skip's car.

Rick called out: "None of you leave this island! I may have questions."

"Were would we go?" Mel asked. "Shotgun!"

Skip started the car and took a U-turn to avoid the police roadblock. He headed back down Fleming Street. "Where to, *mi compadres*?"

Dan pointed ahead. "Take a left up here."

"Roger that," Skip said as he took a quick left onto Simonton Street.

"Go down here and take a left onto Catherine," Dan directed. "I just want to run by Stacey's house real quick, and then I'll buy you a drink at Red's"

"Stacey is Mel's sister, I presume."

"Yeah," Dan replied.

Mel sat quietly in the front seat staring out at the passing houses as the Thing puttered along.

"How long has she been missing?" Skip asked.

"We're not sure," Dan replied. "She hadn't been to see Mel in over three weeks, but we don't know exactly when she went missing. Her neighbors don't remember the last time they saw her."

"Dan will find her," Mel said. "Right, Dan?"

Dan patted Mel on the shoulder. "That's right, pal, we'll find her."

Skip slowed at the flashing yellow light at the corner of Grinnell and Catherine, next to Old Town Self Storage. He looked both ways and rolled through the intersection.

"We should get my car," Mel stated.

"Dude, where's your car?" Skip asked with a Spicoli-esque crackle.

"It's at th—"

Dan interrupted. "He doesn't have a car."

"Where is her house?" Skip asked.

"Right up here."

Skip slowed as they went by Stacey's house. "What are we looking for?"

"I have no idea," Dan answered.

All three men looked at the house as Skip drove by. Nothing had changed. The car still sat in the driveway with the windows down, and the house was dark.

"Where are you, Stacey?" Mel whispered.

Skip turned the corner at Watson Street and made a bee-line for Red's.

Chapter Thirty-One

Dan, Mel and Skip sat at the bar. Mel studied the wine list once again, as Red made a tequila, Seven, and Lime for Dan, and a vodka martini up, dry, and dirty for Skip.

"I can't believe you went without me," Red complained.

"You said you were busy," Dan said, looking around the room. "But it doesn't look like you are."

"We were slammed at dinner time." Red slid Dan his drink.

"Slammed?" Dan asked with doubt in his tone.

Red pushed Skip's drink across the bar. "Okay, the truth is, we were dead, but there was this blond sitting here earlier." Red cupped his hands out in front of him. "A big girl."

Skip held his hand in the air. "Up high, Red man!"

Red high-fived him. "See anything you like on that wine list, Mel?"

"I think I'll have the water."

"Comin' up."

"So, you thought you had a chance with some broad tonight, so you lied and said you couldn't make it?" Dan asked.

"That's exactly right," Red answered. "And you would have done the same thing."

Dan nodded in agreement. "You're probably right. So, where is she now," he asked, looking around hopefully.

Red gave Mel his water. "It's a funny story."

"Can't wait to hear it," Dan said.

Skip sipped his martini. "Me too, Red man," he agreed.

Dan downed his drink in two gulps and pushed his glass back toward Red.

Red began his story as he made Dan another drink. "She came in, and all heads turned."

Dan cocked his head. "All heads? You mean four heads, including yours?"

"Listen dick head, let me tell my story."

"Yeah, let him tell his story, Dan," Mel said.

"So she walks in, long curly blond hair, tight jeans, and bursting out of a pink halter top, and comes right up to the bar, sits down and orders a glass of white wine. I pour her a glass. She looks around and says, 'Nice place, you the owner?' I say, 'Yes, I am.' Then she tells me I'm kinda cute."

"Did she have her seeing eye dog with her?" Dan asked.

Skip chuckled but Red ignored the jab. "Anyway," he continued, "while we're talking I noticed she was wearing a wedding ring. I say, 'Are you married?' She says, 'Yes, does it matter?' Now, under normal circumstances I would have said yes, but she was not a normal circumstance. So I say, 'I guess not.'"

Dan looked at the clock over the bar. "Are you going to tell this whole story in real time?"

"Shh!" Skip said.

"Thank you, Skip," Red said. "We talk for about half an hour and then this old guy comes in, probably in his early sixties, good-looking guy, great shape."

"So, then you fell in love with the guy?" Dan asked.

"Shh!" Mel said.

"This guy comes up to the bar and sits down right next to her. Long story short—"

"Thank God."

"Turns out the guy is her husband, and he wants me to come over tonight."

"For what?" Mel asked.

"You know," Red answered.

"I have no idea," Mel said.

"He wants to watch Red and his wife," Skip offered. "Or maybe even join in the fun."

"Watch them what?" Mel asked.

"Have sex, for Chrissakes!" Dan shouted.

"Huh!" Mel said. "And they call me crazy."

"What time are ya going over?" Skip asked.

"I'm not. Would you do something like that?" Red asked.

Skip took another sip. "If I had a dollar, dude."

Red laughed and then turned his attention to Dan. "So, did you guys find anything at Lonnie's apartment?"

Dan reached into his pocket and pulled out his money clip. Handing a five dollar bill to Mel he said, "Why don't you go over and play some music on the jukebox?"

Mel snatched the five. "Good idea."

"Some Jimmy Buffett," Dan requested.

"And some Kenny Chesney," Red said.

"And some Marley," Skip threw in.

"Coming right up," Mel announced as he jumped from his bar stool.

"We didn't find anything," Dan said, responding to Red's earlier question. "The apartment was empty—doors locked, and no sign of a scuffle."

"Except for the dead dude," Skip corrected.

"What dead dude?" Red asked.

"When we got in the apartment, Lonnie was on the floor and his brains were on the wall," Dan explained.

Red winced. "Ouch. Suicide?"

Skip shook his head. "No, there was no weapon at the scene."

Red asked, "Call the cops?"

"Yup," Dan answered.

"Chief Carver was pissed," Skip said.

"Told us not to leave the island," Dan said.

"Where would you go?" Red asked.

Skip got up from the bar and ran his fingers through his shoulder-length blond hair. "Well, I better mosey, dudes. I told Tiff I wouldn't be too late. You need a ride home, Dan?"

"I'm sure we can find a ride home. You go ahead and take off, Skip. Thanks for your help."

Skip put up his hand to fist bump. "No problem, Dan the man. Catch ya later, Red man." He turned and headed for the door.

"So what's your next move?" Red asked.

"I have a date with Maxine tomorrow night."

"The nurse?"

"Yup."

"Figures."

"What's that supposed to mean?"

"It's always either a nurse or a waitress."

"That's not true," Dan said. "Karen Hinder was in real estate."

Red grabbed Dan's empty glass. "We don't really know that. She was probably a waitress pretending to be in real estate."

Dan knit his brows and dragged his teeth across his bottom lip. Mel had selected Buffett's "A Pirate Looks At Forty" on the jukebox. How appropriate. "Yeah, you're probably right, everything she said was pretty much a lie."

Red slid the refreshed glass across the bar. "Don't worry, pal, you'll get it right one of these days."

Dan took a big swig. "I had it right once." *Shit, maybe I better slow down.*

Chapter Thirty-Two

It was a little after eleven when the bright yellow cab pulled up in front of 632 Beach View Street. Dan and Mel exited the back seat, each carrying a plastic Winn-Dixie bag. The twenty-something driver rolled down the passenger side window as Dan fumbled for his money clip. He pulled a fifty from the clip and tossed it through the window and onto the seat. "You want your change, Mr. Coast?" the driver asked.

Dan waved his hand. "Keep it, Griff, and thanks for waiting at the store ... and tell your mom I said hi."

"Thanks, Mr. Coast, I'll tell her."

The cab pulled away and sped down the street.

Mel walked up the front steps and pulled back the welcome mat, grabbed the key, unlocked the door, and tossed the key back under the mat. Buddy met them at the door, tail wagging. "You want to watch some television, Dan?" Mel reached down and scratched Buddy on the head.

Dan took the grocery bag from Mel. "Aren't you tired, Mel?"

"I'm wide awake." Mel turned on the TV and flopped down in the La-Z-Boy.

Dan went to the kitchen, set the bags on the counter, grabbed Mel's medication from the cupboard over the sink, and poured him a glass of water. When he returned to the living room he said, "Here, take these."

Mel took the pills as he was told and washed them down with a big drink of water. "Thanks, Dan."

"You're welcome, Mel."

Mel grabbed Dan's arm as he started to walk away. "I mean for everything … thanks for helping me find my sister, getting me out of that hospital, helping me with my meds. You're a good guy, Dan."

Dan nodded his head. "After I put away the groceries I'm gonna hit the hay, Mel. Maybe you should too."

Mel sat his half-empty glass of water on the end table. "Yeah, maybe you're right. It's been a long day."

Chapter Thirty-Three

When Dan awoke the following morning he couldn't move his feet. *Oh, Christ, I'm paralyzed.* He raised his head and looked to the foot of his bed. Buddy was lying across his feet, sound asleep, and snoring. "Hey!" Dan said. Buddy ignored him. Dan tried to carefully pull his feet out from underneath the dog. Buddy raised his head and gave Dan a *what-the-Christ-are-you-doing?* look.

"Sorry, but you wouldn't move."

Buddy crawled up the bed and lay down next to Dan. Dan reached over and scratched him behind the ears. "What's the matter, pal? You're not usually much of a cuddler."

Buddy snuggled up under Dan's armpit. There was a knock at the bedroom door.

"Yeah?" Dan called out.

"It's me," Mel said.

"I figured."

"Can I come in?"

"Sure." As the door opened Dan shooed Buddy off the bed. "Damn dog always climbs up on the bed."

"You awake?"

"Well, I wasn't talking in my sleep, Mel."

Mel pushed the door open farther and the mouthwatering aroma of bacon rushed in. "I made breakfast."

"Wow! Really? I'll be right out."

Mel backed into the hall and closed the door behind him. Buddy jumped back up on the bed. Dan slipped on yesterday's cargo shorts and picked up a T-shirt that had been lying on the floor for who knows how long. He sniffed the pits, shrugged, and put it on. "Come on, dog, let's see what Mel has done to the kitchen."

Dan exited the hall into the dining room. The *Key West Citizen* lay on the table. *Walker, Texas Ranger* was on the television. He went into the kitchen. Mel stood in front of the stove, his cardboard badge hung around his neck.

"Smells good," Dan said.

Mel scooped the scrambled eggs onto a plate with a wooden spoon. "I hope you like scrambled eggs."

"I do."

"You want to eat out back or at the table?"

"Table, I guess."

The toast popped up. Mel opened the cupboard door and took out a mug. "Coffee?"

"Sure."

"You should get a picnic table."

"Yup." Dan turned and went back into the dining room and sat down at the table.

Mel sat the plate of bacon, eggs, and toast in front of Dan, and then the coffee. Then he went back to the kitchen and made his own plate and a glass of water.

Dan took a bite of eggs. "Not bad. In fact, pretty damn good. By the way, Mel, don't you ever drink anything other than water?"

"Not anymore." Mel bit into his toast. "I'm not supposed to drink alcohol or beverages with caffeine, and sugar makes me really hyper, so I just drink water."

"They have decaf coffee and soda, you know. And they also have diet soda with no sugar."

Mel took a drink of his water. "I know, but if I drink diet soda then I wish I had a regular soda, and if I drink decaf coffee then I wish I had a cup of regular coffee. If I just drink water, then I don't have to think about it."

Dan ate some bacon. It was crispy, just like he liked it, and tasted like a slice of heaven. "Damn fine pig," he said, by way of compliment, adding, "If that's the case, why do you always look at the wine list?"

"Because wine was my favorite thing to drink back when I was a cop. I drank a lot of it, too much of it, and if I can look at the wine list, and not order a glass, then I'm strong enough to make it through another day."

Dan furrowed his brow. Mel's reasoning made no sense to Dan what so ever. "Makes sense ... I guess," he said.

Mel stared at his plate for a moment and then said, "What's our next move?"

Dan shrugged. "I have a couple phone calls to make, and I asked Skip to look into a couple things for me, so we'll wait and see if he turns up anything. Also, we'll stop over to the police station later this afternoon and see if Carver's had any luck. Until then, I guess we'll just hang around here."

"Will Chief Carver tell you if he does find something?" Mel asked.

"If he wants us to answer any of *his* questions, then he'll have to answer some of ours."

"It doesn't seem like he likes you very much."

"Not much anymore," Dan agreed. He shoved the last bite of eggs into his mouth, stood, grabbed his newspaper and coffee and went for the back door. "I'll be out back reading the paper if you need me."

Mel looked around the table. "Um... okay, I guess I'll clean up then."

Chapter Thirty-Four

Lonnie Rook was front page, above the fold news. The headline read LOCAL MAN FOUND DEAD IN HIS APARTMENT. Lonnie's unflattering hospital ID photo accompanied the article. Dan already knew the story but he read it anyway, and then turned to the third page where the story continued. He almost felt bad after reading the article … almost. Dan refolded the paper and laid it on the ground next to his chair. He pulled his phone from his pocket, tapped the screen, and put it to his ear.

"Yes?"

"Maxine, it's Dan."

"I know."

"You still at work?"

"Till four."

"Can you do me a big favor?"

"Sure."

"I need you to sneak Mel's file out of the hospital."

There was a long pause and then Maxine said, "Is that why you asked me out tonight, Dan?"

"No, Maxine, but I need this. I gotta look into Mel's history, find out where he came from, who he was before. It's the only way I can help him. Can you do this for me?"

"I can't take the file, Dan, but I'll copy everything that's in it for you."

"Thanks, Maxine. I'll see you at six. Bye."

"Bye."

Dan hung up the phone and dropped it on the paper. The back door slammed shut.

"Kitchen's clean," Mel said, and made his way down to the other Adirondack chair to have a seat.

"Good man. There'll be a little something extra in your paycheck this week."

"I get a paycheck?"

Dan shook his head. "No."

"I knew it was too good to be true." Mel sat. "What's next?"

"It's your call, Mel. I don't have anything to do till I have to get ready for my date."

"How about if we build a picnic table?"

"You want to build a picnic table?"

"Yeah, everyone should have a picnic table and you don't have one. Do you have tools?"

Dan pointed to the woodshed. "The shed is full of tools."

"Perfect! After you finish your coffee we'll ask Bev if we can borrow her minivan and then we'll head over to Manley's for materials."

"Bev doesn't want us loading lumber in her minivan," Dan said.

Bev's back door slammed shut. "There she is now," Mel said excitedly. "I'll ask her."

"No!"

"Hey, beautiful Bev!" Mel yelled. "Can we use your van to run to Manley's and get materials for a picnic table? Dan and I are going to build one today."

Bev hollered back, "Sure, Mel that would be fine."

"Thanks, beautiful Bev. I told Dan you wouldn't mind." Mel turned to Dan. "I knew she wouldn't care. Now go get ready so we can get this project started."

Dan climbed out of his chair. "Fine."

Mel slapped his hands together. "This is going to be awesome! I love building things."

"Yeah, I bet you and power tools are a great combination," Dan grumbled as he walked up the gravel pathway to the back door.

Chapter Thirty-Five

Dan backed Bev's minivan out of her driveway and started down the street.

"I don't know why you won't let me drive," Mel said.

Dan looked over. "You really don't know, Mel?"

"Is it because I'm crazy?"

"No, it's because you don't have a driver's license."

Dan swung a left onto Ashby Street.

"I used to have one."

"Well, when you get another one, let me know, and I'll let you drive."

"Can we swing by the Motor Vehicle Department?"

"No."

Dan took a right on Flagler Avenue.

"Then how am I going to get a driver's license?"

"It's Saturday, the Motor Vehicle Department isn't open on Saturday."

"Are you busy on Monday?"

"Just drop it, Mel."

Mel leaned his head on the passenger side window. "Fine."

Dan reached down and turned on the radio. It was already tuned to US-1, 104.1, the popular classic hits station. Dire Straits were playing *Sultans of Swing*. He took a left onto Kennedy Drive.

"You like this song?" Dan asked.

Mel's head was still leaning against the window. "No."

Dan jerked the wheel right and then quickly back, smacking Mel's head against the window with a thud. "Oh, sorry, pal, there was a squirrel in the road."

Mel rubbed the side of his head. "You're a dick."

"Well, stop acting like a little baby. After we find your sister we'll look into getting your driver's license."

"Then can I get my Ferrari out of storage?"

Dan shook his head. "Yeah, and then you, me, Rick, and T.C. will take it for a drive around the island."

"It's only a two-seater."

"Oh, yeah, how stupid of me."

Dan pulled the minivan into the Home Depot parking lot and found a parking space close to the door.

"This isn't Manley's," Mel commented.

"No kidding?" Dan asked sarcastically.

"I wanted to go to Manley's."

"I didn't."

The two men got out and walked toward the door. As they walked under the canopy, Mel said, "We should have parked under here, it's a lot closer."

"This isn't a parking spot. It's for loading materials."

Mel looked around. "How come these guys are parked under here then?" he asked, pointing at the three trucks parked close by.

"Because they're assholes, and they're too goddamn lazy to walk from the parking lot," Dan answered matter-of-factly.

A fourth truck pulled under the canopy and a brawny mountain of a man got out. Dan instantly thought of Clint Walker, the rugged TV and movie star of yore. The sleeves of his T-shirt could barely contain his biceps.

"Hey, asshole, this isn't a parking lot, it's for loading materials," Mel called out.

The man slammed the door of his pickup. "What did you say?"

Mel pulled his cardboard badge out from under his shirt and let it drop against his chest. "You heard me, fella." He threw a thumb over his shoulder. "The parking lot is out *there*. This under *here* is for loading and unloading only."

The man walked up to Mel and Dan. He was a least six inches taller and outweighed them by fifty pounds. "You got some kinda death wish or something?"

Dan got between the two men. "He didn't mean anything. He thought you were someone else."

Mel pulled his small note pad and pen from his back pocket. "I'm going to need your name, tough guy."

With a sweep of his arm the man effortlessly knocked Dan to ground and then grabbed Mel by the shirt, lifting him off his feet. Dan quickly jumped to his feet and leapt on the man's back putting his arm around his throat in a choke hold. The tough guy let go of Mel.

Mel took two steps back and then kicked the man in the balls, dropping him to his knees with Dan still on his back. "The bigger they are, the harder they fall," he said.

Dan climbed off the man's back and then, with his foot, shoved him to the ground.

The man lay on the concrete clutching the family jewels and moaning. "I'll get you bastards for this," he groaned hoarsely. A knot of bystanders had started to congregate.

Dan headed back toward the van. "Come on."

Mel followed. "But I have to fill out a report."

"Forget it and just come on." Dan said as he hurried along.

"Where are we going? What about the picnic table?"

Dan jumped back in the van. Mel did the same. Dan started the engine and hauled ass out of the parking lot.

"Why did we leave?"

"Because I didn't want to be there when that hulking son of a bitch got back up."

"Are you scared of him?"

"You bet your ass, I'm scared of him!"

"Where are we going now?"

"Manley's"

"Good idea."

Chapter Thirty-Six

Dan found a decent parking space at Manley deBoer Lumber Company, and the two men entered the building, this time without incident.

They walked up to the sales counter.

"Can I help you?" the gentleman behind the counter asked.

"We just need twelve eight-foot two-by-sixes and four eight-foot two-by-fours," Dan responded.

The man began poking at the keyboard in front of him.

"Treated?"

"Nope."

"Cash or credit?"

Dan pulled his money clip from his pocket. "Cash."

"That will be $72.84 and you can pull your truck around to the side door."

Dan paid the man, and he and Mel returned to the van.

"How come you didn't get any nails?"

Dan started the van. "I have plenty of nails."

"Do you have two hammers?"

"Probably, but we're using my nail gun so we won't need any hammers."

"I never used a nail gun before."

Dan backed up to the overhead door at the end of the building. "Well, I guess this is your lucky day."

Dan grabbed the receipt off of the dashboard as they exited the van. A young man in jeans and a blue T-shirt approached them, smiling broadly.

"What can I get for you today?" the young man asked pleasantly.

Dan held up his receipt. "A few two-by-fours and—"

"Hey, Steve!" Mel interrupted.

Dan glanced over at Mel and then back at the young man, who was now wearing a look of fear and surprise.

Steve spun and started running in the opposite direction.

"I take it you know that guy?" Dan asked.

"That's Steve. He's my sister's boyfriend," Mel answered matter-of-factly.

"Boyfriend? What the Christ?" Dan handed the receipt to Mel and gave chase. "Hey! We just want to talk to you!" he called out as Steve rounded the corner and exited through a side door into the parking lot.

Ship of Fools

When Dan got to the door he looked in every direction. Then he saw Steve climbing into a blue, late model Chevy Malibu in the employee parking area.

Steve slammed the car in reverse, as he was still rolling backwards, he forced it into drive and floored it, squealing the tires and kicking up dirt and pebbles all over the side of the building.

Dan started running after the car but stopped in the middle of the parking lot and watched as Steve sped down Frances Street, running the stop sign and sliding around the corner onto Eaton Street. *Son of a bitch.*

Dan turned and walked back to the van, still huffing and puffing from his short sprint.

"Did you catch him?" Mel asked, loading the last two-by-fours into the van with the help of another Manley's associate.

"No."

Mel shut the back hatch. "Wow, you're really out of shape." He pulled the receipt from his pants pocket.

"Yeah, I know," Dan answered, ripping the receipt from Mel's hand. "You don't think you should have let me know that your sister had a boyfriend and that he worked *here*."

Mel opened the passenger side door. "That's why I wanted to come here and not Home Depot."

"You could have told me that's why you wanted to come here!" Dan slammed his door.

"Are you sure I didn't mention it to you?"

Dan started the car and threw it into drive. "Yeah, pretty sure."

"Huh, I could have sworn I said something. Oh well, let's get this picnic table built."

Chapter Thirty-Seven

After the lumber was stacked in the backyard and Bev's van had been returned to her driveway, Dan ran an extension cord from his kitchen, through the screen door, and lastly to his air compressor. His saw horses were unfolded, and a few two-by-sixes lay on top of them.

Dan exited the woodshed carrying his circular saw. "Do you have any idea where this Steve lives?" he asked.

"He lives here in Key West somewhere," Mel answered.

"That's a big help."

"Sorry, I've never been to his house. The only times I've met him is when he came with my sister to visit me at the hospital."

"Mel, how long did you and your sister live here before you went to live at the hospital?"

"I don't *live* at the hospital, Dan; I'm just staying there for a while."

"Okay, then how long did you live here before you went to *stay* at the hospital for a while?"

Mel thought for a second. "Maybe two or three weeks."

Dan went back to the woodshed and got out his nail gun. He flipped on the compressor and plugged the hose into the end of the gun. He laid the gun on the ground next to the air compressor and returned to the shed. When he came back out Mel was holding the gun.

"I bet one of these nails would go right through someone's skull," Mel commented, as he inspected the gun and then pointed it out toward the beach.

Dan's eyes widened. "Um, maybe it's time for your medication." He reached down and unplugged the compressor and disconnected the hose. "We don't want any accidents." He took the gun from Mel and laid it back on the ground.

"Well, in the movies when they shoot these guns at people, the nails stick right in their heads." He illustrated this grim demise by shooting his finger at his noggin, crossing his eyes, and sticking out his tongue.

"That's only in the movies, Mel."

"Yeah, *a lot of movies,* so it must really work," Mel argued.

Dan reached down, picked up the gun, and plugged it back into the hose. He pointed the gun toward the beach and pulled the trigger. "See, nothing happens."

"Huh, I wonder why it works in the movies." Mel asked sadly.

Dan pulled the trigger again and slammed the tip of the gun against one of the two-by-fours. *Bang!* "See, you have to hit the gun against something for it to work."

Mel nodded. "Good to know."

Dan unplugged the gun. "So, keep that in mind if you ever find yourself in some cheap cliché action film." Dan went to the house to get Mel's medication.

When Dan returned, he had the pills and a glass of water in one hand, and a drink he had made for himself in the other. "Here," he said, handing Mel his drink.

"Thanks."

Dan took a sip of his drink and set it down on the ground. He then went back to the shed for a pencil and tape measure. "How long has your sister been dating Steve?

"A long time. More than a year, I guess."

"Do you think he might be hiding her somewhere?"

"Maybe. He's a really nice guy."

Dan checked his cell phone for the time. "We better get this thing going."

"Where are the plans?" Mel asked, looking around.

"Plans? We don't need any plans. It's a picnic table for Chrissakes. I could build it with my eyes closed."

Dan measured one of the boards and put a mark at thirty-six inches.

"Are you going to let me use the nail gun?" Mel asked.

Dan picked up his combination square. "Yes. If you quit bugging me about it."

"Okay."

"Can I use the saw?"

"No."

"Why?"

"Because I don't want to bring you back to the hospital with only one arm."

"They would probably be pissed."

Dan measured another board. "What's Steve's last name?"

"Durkin."

"It will be easy enough to find out where he lives. Hand me the saw, but don't pull the trigger."

Mel picked up the saw and pulled the trigger. "Wow! I bet that could cut someone's head off."

Dan grabbed the saw. "Jesus Christ! How long does it take for those meds to kick in?"

Chapter Thirty-Eight

Dan laid the last two-by-six across the bench supports. "Here, put two nails in this end and then two nails in that end."

Mel smacked the tip of the nail gun against the board twice. *Bang! Bang!* Then he did the same at the other end. "There, all done."

Dan and Mel both stepped back to admire their work. "Looks good."

"Now we just have to paint it," Mel remarked.

"Maybe tomorrow. We better get this stuff picked up. I've got to get ready to pick up Maxine."

"You go ahead and get ready," Mel said. "I'll get the tools picked up."

"Sounds like a plan." Dan pivoted on one foot and headed up the gravel pathway to the back door.

Ship of Fools

*****

When Dan exited the hallway into the living room Mel was sitting in the La-Z-Boy, watching *Sanford and Son*. A glass of water sat on the end table next to him. He looked over at Dan.

"Well, don't you look nice," Mel observed. "Hair combed. You even shaved! You barely look like a bum."

"Thanks." Dan went to the bar to make himself a drink. "What are ya watching?"

"Sanford and Son. The one where Fred and Lamont try to move a piano for a prissy antique dealer—"

"—and he makes them where those elf slippers." Dan finished for him as he poured a shot of tequila into a glass. "Classic."

"They don't make 'em like this anymore," Mel agreed.

"You want something to eat before I leave?"

"No. Bev and I are ordering out. Probably watch a movie or something."

"What time are you going over?"

"Six."

"Did you get those tools picked up?"

"Not yet, but I will."

Dan downed the shot of tequila and made his way toward the door. "Well, I better get going."

"You have a condom?" Mel called out.

"No, I don't have a condom. Jesus!"

Dan closed the door behind him, but not before he heard Mel yell, "Don't be silly, wrap your willy!"

Chapter Thirty-Nine

At two minutes before six Dan turned right off of White Street onto Newton Street. He slowed and read the house numbers as he passed each house. About five houses up he came to Maxine's and pulled the pink Volkswagen Bug to the curb. He checked the time on the radio. Perfect.

Like a pat of toothpaste, Dan squeezed his good-sized frame out of the tight little nutshell of a car. He remembered reading somewhere that the Beetle was Hitler's idea. Figures. The last laugh of the worst human being of all time. Still, he had to admire the bugs reliability—notwithstanding the engine in the damn trunk.

"Nice car, buddy!" he heard someone shout. He looked over and saw two construction workers laughing as they climbed into their truck. Dan thought about yelling something back, but who would have the last laugh? After all he was driving a *pink* car.

Maxine opened the front door before Dan got to the porch. *Eager,* he thought, *or does she just not want me in her house?*

"Right on time," Maxine said.

"My punctuality is second only to my good looks and snappy wit," Dan returned.

"Hadn't really noticed the wit."

Maxine was dressed in white capris, white flip-flops and a red, see-through, flowered top. Underneath the top she wore a red tank-top. Her hair was pulled back into a ponytail. She was carrying a large manila file folder.

Dan walked around to the passenger side of the car and opened the door.

"I didn't picture you as a door opener," Maxine said.

Dan smiled and shut the door.

When Dan climbed into the car Maxine handed him the folder. "This is Mel's entire file."

Dan opened the folder and flipped through the pages. "Thanks, I'll take a look at this later." Dan reached back and placed the folder on the back seat, started the car, and pulled away from the curb.

"So, where are you taking me?"

Dan took a right onto Eisenhower Street. "I thought we could have dinner and then after, if we felt like it, maybe we could see a movie or something."

"Dinner and a movie, that's original. Did you come up with that on your own?"

"Hey give me a break, I don't date that much."

"I'm just joking with you."

"How about you?"

"How about me, what?"

"Do you date a lot?"

"I go out with my friends a few times a month, but I haven't been on a date in"—Maxine thought for a second__"—probably a year."

Dan found that hard to believe. "Wow, really? Why is that?"

"Mostly my work schedule. Also, I was taking classes up until the first part of January."

Dan waited at the stop light and then turned right onto Truman Avenue. "*College* classes?" he asked.

"Yes. I was an LPN for ten years, and then I decided to go back to school for my RN."

Dan was trying to figure Maxine's approximate age in his head. *Let's see, graduated at eighteen, two years of college, worked as an LPN for ten years, then back to school for maybe two years… thirty-two, maybe.*

"What are you thinking about?"

"Nothing." Dan swung a right onto Whitehead Street.

"So, how is Mel doing?"

"Good. Gotta stay on top of those meds though, he gets some weird ideas when they start to wear off. Then he starts rubbing that ear and flicking those fingers together."

Maxine laughed. "Yeah, meds are important."

"Maybe we can swing by the house later and you can take a look at him … make sure you think he's okay."

"Now, there's a line no one has ever used on me before: 'Wanna come on back to my place and check on my mental patient?'"

"I know *I've* never used that line before." Dan pulled to the curb and shut off the engine.

"Did you leave him alone for the night?"

"Christ no! I left him with a neighbor, a friend of mine." Dan clambered out of the bug and walked around to open Maxine's door. She climbed out with far more ease, and together they walked up the sidewalk and around the corner onto Caroline Street to a gate in a white picket fence.

A woman standing behind the gate said, "How are you folks this evening?"

"Wonderful," Dan said. "How are you?"

"I'm good. Did you have reservations?"

"Yes. Dan Coast."

The hostess ran her finger down the page of a guestbook and made a check mark next to the name Coast. "Right this way."

Dan and Maxine followed the hostess to their table on the patio. She pulled out one of the chairs. "Is this good?" she asked.

"Fantastic," Dan responded and they sat down.

"Your waitress tonight will be Lydia. She'll be right with you."

"Thank you," Maxine said, and opened the drink menu. Dan did the same.

Dan scanned the page, already knowing that he wanted tequila. *Maybe I should just have a soda*, he thought. *Yeah, I'll just have a soda and then I'll have a real drink later if we stop somewhere. No need to start right in drinking. I'll just have a soda.*

"Hi, my name is Lydia. Can I get you a drink?"

Maxine spoke first. "I'll have a Captain and Coke, please."

Lydia jotted it down in her pad. "And for you, sir?"

Soda, I'll have soda. "I'll have a tequila, Seven, and lime, please." *Dammit!*

"Okay, I'll be right back with those and to take your order."

Dan nodded and opened his menu. "Should we order an appetizer?"

Maxine scanned the page. "Sure."

"See anything you like?"

"These shrimp and bacon quesadillas sound good."

"Yes they do," Dan agreed.

The waitress returned with the drinks and took their order. Maxine ordered the yellow tail snapper. Dan ordered the jerked chicken. When the waitress turned and went back inside Dan made a conscious effort not to stare at her ass.

"So, do you live alone?" Dan asked.

"No. Who could afford it? I have two roommates, Megan and Shauna. Megan tends bar and Shauna is a receptionist at the hospital. Shauna owns the house; she got it when her and her husband divorced a few years back."

Dan sipped his drink and leaned back in his chair. "And I guess you know *my* roommate."

Maxine laughed. "All too well. Where did you say he was tonight?"

"He's watching a movie and eating pizza at my neighbor's house."

"A woman?" Maxine asked.

"Yes, and it was hard convincing him that it wasn't a date."

"I bet. Mel is quite the ladies' man."

"I've noticed."

"When I first started working at the hospital, he referred to me as Marvelous Maxine."

Lydia sat their plates in front of them. "Is there anything else I can get for you?" she asked.

"I'll have another drink, please," Maxine answered.

"Same here," Dan said. *Last one*, he thought.

Chapter Forty

After dinner, Dan and Maxine walked back to the car. Once again Dan opened Maxine's door for her. "Thank you," she said, and climbed in. Dan nodded and shut the door.

When Dan got in the car, he turned to Maxine. "It's still pretty early. Did you want to see a movie or grab a drink somewhere?"

"I wouldn't mind seeing a movie," Maxine answered. "What's playing?"

Dan pulled away from the curb. "I have no idea. I haven't been to the movies in over a year."

"You don't like going to the movies?"

"I love going to the movies. I just hate going alone."

"You don't go with your friends?"

"Red won't go to the movies with me anymore because I won't let him leave a seat empty between us."

Maxine laughed. "Yeah, why do guys do that?"

Dan made a quick U-turn. "Insecurity. They're afraid someone might think they're gay."

"Are you serious?"

"Last time we went to the movies he sat down first, so I sat down right next to him. He said, 'Move over one seat, people are going to think we're gay'."

"Did you move over one?"

"No. I put my arm around him and gave him a big kiss on the cheek. And that was the last time he went to the movies with me."

Laughing, Maxine gazed out the window as they drove past The Green Parrot Bar. She pointed out the window. "You ever go there?"

"Never been," Dan responded.

"Really? How long have you lived here?"

"A few years," Dan answered. They drove by The Ernest Hemingway Home. Dan shook his head before Maxine could ask. "Nope, never been there either." He took a left onto Catherine Street.

"Where are we going?"

"I just wanted to drive by Mel's sister's house one more time." Dan told Maxine the story about seeing Stacey Gormin's boyfriend at the lumber yard, and how he ran from them.

Dan slowed at the flashing light at the corner of Catherine and Grinnell.

"So, what's the story behind this car?" Maxine asked.

"I'm between cars right now, had a little accident in mine awhile back. I'm borrowing this one till I buy another one." Dan pulled to the curb in front of Stacey's house.

"Is she just a friend?"

Dan looked at each window in the house not knowing exactly what he was looking for, and then he pulled forward and looked down between the houses. "Is who just a friend?"

"The woman you borrowed the car from."

Dan laughed. "It's not a woman. The car belongs to Red."

Maxine's red lips curled into a smirk. "Wait a minute, he won't sit next to you in the movie theater for fear that someone might think he's gay, but he's fine with driving a pink Volkswagen Bug with a bumper sticker on the back that says *Mafia Wife*?"

Dan slowly pulled away from the curb. "He's a walking enigma."

"I guess so."

"What made you ask about the car, anyway?" Dan asked.

"When we drove by the self-storage place back there, some guys were covering a car with a big tarp, and it got me wondering why a private eye such as yourself didn't have a car like that."

"I'm not a private eye," Dan responded. Then his curiosity got the best of him. "What kind of car was it?"

"One of those hot shit Italian sports cars, a red one, you know like Tom Selleck drove on *Magnum*."

Dan slammed on the brakes. "A Ferrari?"

"Yeah, a Ferrari."

Dan spun the tires, making another U-turn, and sped back to Old Town Storage.

"What's the matter?" Maxine asked.

"I'm not sure," Dan responded, skidding to a stop across from the gate. A single dim floodlight mounted on the storage building inadequately illuminated the property. Dan's eyes scanned the yard. "Which car was it?" he inquired.

Maxine pointed. "The one right there on the end."

"How many guys were in the yard?"

"Two."

Dan glanced at the time on the dashboard. "I wonder what time they leave."

Maxine motioned toward the front of the building. "Looks like someone is leaving now."

Dan looked to the front of the building to see two men exiting through the front door. One man climbed into a dark-colored truck while the other man slid closed, and locked the front door of the building. When he was finished he too climbed into the truck, backed it out of the parking lot, and sped off down Grinnell Street.

"I gotta get a closer look at that car," Dan said.

"There's probably security cameras," Maxine pointed out.

"I know, but it's dark … and I'm not stealing anything, so they probably won't even look at the security tapes." Dan opened the door. "Wait here."

"Well, I wasn't going with you."

Dan shut the door and ran stealthily across the street. When he got to the gate he looked around the yard, then up the street one way and down the other. There was no one in sight. He jumped up on the fence and climbed over; he wished Mel were around to see firsthand he was still pretty spry for an aging white guy. He ran to the first car and pulled back the tarp. There it was, a Ferrari F355.

Ship of Fools

Holy shit! That nut was telling the truth. This is way better than Magnum's. This car was a convertible and almost twenty-five years newer that Magnum's. Dan swore he felt something move in his pants.

Dan went around to the back of the car, lifted the tarp, and looked at the license plate. He felt his pockets for a pen. Nothing. He pulled out his phone and called Maxine.

"Hello?"

"It's Dan."

"I know."

"I need a pen."

"Hold on." Maxine hung up the phone and searched through her purse for a pen. She found one, ran across the street and met Dan at the gate. She passed the pen through the chain link fence. "This is exciting!"

Dan took the pen. "Yeah, I think I peed myself a little," he said sarcastically.

Maxine ran back to the Bug.

Dan went back to the rear of the car and jotted down the plate number on his hand. When he was finished he jumped back over the fence and returned to the car.

"What's next?" Maxine asked.

"We go to the movies."

Chapter Forty-One

"Holy shit!" Dan said as they exited the theater, where *Interstellar* had drawn a packed house, and walked across the parking lot. "Three hours long. Movies should never be longer than ninety minutes."

"Yeah, that's a long time to sit there," Maxine agreed.

"And I don't know about you, but even when McConaughey's wearing a space suit, I just keep waiting for him to say, 'I get older, they stay the same age.'"

Maxine laughed. "I know, or, 'All right, all right, all right,'" Maxine said in her best McConaughey impression.

Dan was impressed. "Hey, that's pretty damn good."

"I try."

The two laughed together as Dan pulled his cell phone from his pocket. "Four missed calls in the last ten minutes," he said.

Maxine opened her purse and looked at her cell. "I've got two missed calls."

Dan checked his call log. "Three from Bev and one from Red."

"Both of my missed calls are from Dr. Richards. Maybe I better call him back, might be important."

Dan dialed Bev's number. It went straight to voice mail; he didn't leave a message. He hung up and called Red.

"Yeah," Red answered.

"You call me?"

"Obviously. I got a call from Bev about fifteen minutes ago. She said she heard something outside and when she looked out the window she saw someone in your yard. She said Mel went out to have a look. I'm on my way over right now."

Dan hung up his phone and dropped it back in his pocket. "Come on," he said to Maxine. "We have to meet Red at my house."

"Yeah," Maxine agreed. "I just got off the phone with Richards. He said two guys were at the hospital tonight asking about Mel."

"He say who they were?"

"They said they were cops. Richards said they had badges but they didn't act like cops."

Dan and Maxine climbed into the car, but this time Dan forgot to open Maxine's door. "Did he say what kind of questions they asked?"

"I guess they just asked what room he was in," Maxine responded. "They said they wanted to ask him a few questions about an old case he had worked on in Los Angeles."

Dan gave her a sideways look. "An old case?"

Maxine shrugged.

"What the hell is going on here?" Dan asked. "First we find a Ferrari that may be Mel's, and now someone's asking about an old case of his."

"Search me," said Maxine, "but I do love a good mystery."

"You and me both."

Dan pulled from the parking lot, took a right, and headed down Northside Drive.

*****

Dan shut off the headlights and coasted to a stop in front of Mrs. McGee's house. He glanced over, and of course she was looking out of her front window. *Neighborhood watch, 24/7 surveillance,* he thought. "Wait here."

"By myself?" Maxine asked.

"Lock the doors when I get out and don't unlock them till I come back."

Dan thought about his pistol tucked away in a black duffle bag below the floor boards in his closet as he bolted across the street, past Red's Firebird, to Bev's house. He ran up to the living room window on the right side of the house and peeked inside, no one in sight. He quietly made his way around to the back of the house, walked up on the deck, and looked in the screen door. A miserable-looking Red was sitting in one of the kitchen chairs, his hands tied around the frame with a dish towel.

Dan put his face close to the screen and let out a, "Psst."

Red's head turned. "Dan?"

"Yeah," Dan whispered. "How are you doing?"

"Oh, wonderful. How the hell do you think I'm doing? I'm tied to a goddamn chair. Get in here and untie me."

Dan went in. "Are you alone?"

"Yeah. They just left a few minutes ago."

Dan untied his friend. "What happened?"

Red stood and rubbed his wrists and opened and closed his hands a few times to get the blood flowing.

"When I got here, I came through the front door. There were two guys with guns here in the kitchen with Bev and Mel. Clean-cut dudes, dressed nice. When they heard me they turned around, and Mel ran out the back door. One of the guys went after him, and the other grabbed Bev and put his gun to her head. He told her to sit down, and then he tied me up. He told me to sit here and not make a sound. Warned me not to call the cops. Then he grabbed Bev by the arm and went out the back door. A few seconds later I heard a car speed away."

"Shit! I wonder where they took them?"

Mel walked through the back door. His clothes were dirty, his shirt was ripped, and he had blood on his face. "They didn't take *me* anywhere."

"Where's Bev?" Dan asked.

"I don't know, the one guy took her in his car," Mel answered.

"Where's the other guy that went after *you*," Red asked.

"He's dead."

"Dead?" Dan blurted out.

"Yeah, Dan. Remember how you told me to put the tools away?"

"Yeah."

"Well, I didn't. And remember how you told me that killing someone with a nail gun could only happen in the movies?"

"Yes?"

"Well, you were wrong."

Dan cringed and thought back to every action film he had ever seen. "You shot the guy in the head with a nail gun?"

"Of course not," Mel answered. The compressor wasn't plugged in … so I beat him over the head with it."

Red tried to hide his amusement. "Where is he?"

"Dan's backyard."

Dan pointed at the flashlight sitting on the top of Bev's refrigerator. "Grab that light and let's take a look. Lead the way, Mel."

In Dan's backyard, Red pointed the flashlight at the lifeless body that lay next to the air compressor. The clean shaven man's short hair was neatly trimmed, and he wore a dark suit. The wound on the side of his head told Dan that there was no reason to check for a pulse.

"Jesus Christ!" Dan said. "How hard did you hit him?"

"I'm guessing *too* hard," Red commented.

"It all happened so fast," said Mel, reliving the struggle animatedly. "He tackled me, and when I turned over he was pulling a gun out of his jacket. I saw the nail gun lying there on the ground, and I grabbed it and swung. I only hit him once."

"Where's the gun?" Red asked, shining the light around the area.

Mel lifted the back of his shirt and pulled the pistol from his waistband. "Right here."

"I think I'll hold on to that for you, Mel," Red said, grabbing the weapon.

Dan pulled the man's jacket open and felt for some identification. He pulled a thin bi-fold wallet out and flipped it open. A photo ID was on the left. On the right, a badge glistened in the glow of the flashlight.

"Shit!" Red said. "He's a cop."

"LAPD. Special Agent Mark Lasko," Dan said.

"They didn't act like cops," Mel commented.

"Yeah, that's what Richards said, too." Dan agreed.

"What are we gonna do with him?" Red asked.

Dan felt the vibration of his phone and snatched it from his pocket. He looked at the screen and saw that it was Bev's cell phone number. He put it on speaker. "Hello?"

"Mr. Coast?"

"Yes."

"I have your friend."

"Well, then, that makes us even, dick head, because we have *your* friend."

"Let me speak to him."

"Agent Lasko can't come to the phone right now, but if you could give *me* the message, I'll be sure that he gets it."

"You have a very wise mouth, Mr. Coast."

Dan grinned. "If I had a dollar. Now tell me, officer, what can I do for you?"

After a slight pause the man began to give Dan instructions. "At ten o'clock tomorrow morning you will deliver Stacey Gormin, Mel Gormin, and Agent Lasko to me. We'll ask the Gormins a few questions and then we'll get what we came here for. If everyone cooperates, Agent Lasko and I will be on our way, and you all will get to live your lives as if this never happened."

"Let me speak to Bev," Dan said.

"I'm sorry, Mr. Coast, Bev can't come to the phone either. She's tied up at the moment."

"Where are we meeting you?" Dan asked defeatedly.

"I'll call you tomorrow morning at nine and give you the location … and Mr. Coast, if you cross me or if I see any cops, I'll kill her, and then I will hunt down and kill all of you, whether you have Agent Lasko or not."

The call ended, Dan looked at his home screen, tapped it a few times, scrolled down, and tapped it again, and then he stuck the phone back in his pocket.

"He's gonna be pissed when he finds out Lasko is dead," Red said.

Dan nodded in agreement. "Let's get him into the woodshed."

Red and Dan lifted Lasko and carried him to the shed, sat him on the floor, and shut the door.

"He's going to start stinking by tomorrow afternoon," Mel said.

"This will all be over tonight," Dan said matter-of-factly.

Red lowered his brow. "How do you figure?"

"Because of a little app called Friend Finder that I downloaded back when Bev was dating that drunken asshole Don Rayburn. Thought it might come in handy someday."

"So, that's why you were doing all that tappin' on your phone a minute ago?" Red said.

"Yep," Dan replied. "Why don't we head in the house, have a drink and come up with a plan."

On the way to the backdoor, Mel asked, "So, how did your date with Maxine go?"

"Oh, shit!" Dan said, and ran for the car.

Chapter Forty-Two

Dan had called a cab to take Maxine home, and then he, Red, and Mel went over the plan they had drawn on a napkin.

"So, what makes you so sure he's at the self-storage building?" Red asked. "That phone app says the signal could be anywhere within two hundred feet of the joint."

"Two reasons," Dan responded. "The red dot is sitting right on *top* of the building, and"—he paused and glared at Mel—"there's a Ferrari parked in the parking lot."

Red glanced over at Mel. "Yours?"

"Yup," Mel answered. "I told you I had a car like Magnum's."

"Sorry I didn't believe you."

"That's okay, Red. I may be nuts, but I'm no liar."

"I'll keep that in mind next time."

"This reminds me of the time my partner, Pete Malloy, and I were working a kidnapping and—"

Dan tapped Mel on the shoulder. "That was *Adam-12*, pal."

Mel looked to the ceiling in thought. "Was it? Huh."

Dan went to his bedroom, opened his closet door, and pulled up the loose floor boards. He reached into the darkness and grabbed the hidden black bag, unzipped it, and removed his gun.

Mel watched as Dan returned to the dining room with the pistol. "Do I get a gun?" he asked.

"Nope," Dan replied.

"You guys have guns."

"That's right," Dan answered, placing the gun in his waistband.

"That's not fair."

"We only have two guns, Mel," Red pointed out.

"If we get another gun, can I have it?"

"Sure," Dan said.

*****

Red pulled his car to the curb at the corner of Grinnell and United and parked. The three men climbed out of the car and began walking toward the storage building.

"So, if we find another gun, I get to keep it, right?" Mel asked once again.

"Yes," Dan whispered. "Now shut up and stop talking about it."

"Just making sure we're on the same page."

When they got to the corner of the building, Skip was already waiting. "Yo! What's up dudes?" Skip raised his arm and high-fived Red and Mel, and then he turned to Dan. "Don't leave me hanging here, Dan the man."

Dan rolled his eyes and halfheartedly slapped the palm of Skip's hand.

"I knew you wanted to, bro," Skip said.

"Okay, listen." Dan turned to Red. "You and Skip are going in through the front door and up the front stairs; Mel and I will go in through the back and up the back stairs."

"Then what?" Skip asked.

"I have no idea," Dan responded. "Just be careful."

"How many are we going up against?" Skip asked.

"Not sure." Dan replied. "There could be two of them. They had a local guy, Manny Delgado, working with them."

"Manny Delgado?" Skip questioned. "That dude don't make a move without his buddy Tank, so there's most likely three of them."

"Tank?" Red asked.

"Tank Portman," Skip answered. "Been friends since they were kids. Tank's not too bright but he's dangerous. Big mother, his name suits him. Just got out of Raiford last month, did ten years for robbery and assault."

"How do you know so much about these guys?" Dan asked.

"Long story," Skip answered cagily. He pulled a revolver from its holster underneath his arm and spun the cylinder. "Let's just get this over with."

Dan pulled out his cell phone and checked the time. "Give us five minutes."

Mel spoke up. "Ten minutes, if you please. I need to check something."

Dan shrugged his shoulders. "Okay then, ten minutes."

Dan and Mel ran stealthily around the building to the side gate. One at a time they each climbed over, jumping to the ground on the other side.

"You did that real good, Dan, for a man getting up in years," Mel observed in his outside voice.

Dan shushed him and started in the direction of the rear entrance.

"Wait!" Mel whispered urgently. He ran to the Ferrari and yanked back the tarp. Dropping to his knees and rolling to his back, he wiggled underneath the car. When he slid back out he was holding a small magnetic box.

"What are you doing?" Dan asked, and then looked around the parking lot.

Mel opened the box, pulled out a key and unlocked the door. "Getting something I need." He opened the door, reached across the seat, and opened the glove box.

"Hurry up."

Mel emerged from the Ferrari's cockpit holding a shoe box. He sat it on the roof of the car, opened it, and pulled out a gold badge that hung from a chain and placed it around his neck. Then he fished under some old photos in the box and filled his hand with a .357 snub nose revolver.

"What the Christ are you gonna do with that cannon?" Dan asked.

Mel pulled the ejector rod and saw that the gun was still loaded, just the way he had left it, and then replaced the cylinder. "I'm going into that building to kill Ranker."

"Ranker?" Dan asked. "Who the hell is Ranker?"

"Lasko's partner. I worked with both of them in Los Angeles. I took something that they thought belonged to them."

"What did you take?"

"Five million dollars in stolen drug money," Mel answered guiltily.

"Holy shit!" Dan said, as a hundred questions ran through his mind. The only one he got out was, "Where's the money now?"

"I'm not sure, I told my sister to hide it. I told her never to tell me where it was because I'm a little crazy."

"Yeah, smart move. But why the hell didn't you mention you knew these guys before now?"

"Because I'm a—"

"Little crazy, yeah, I know," Dan supplied. "Well, you've got your gun now. Happy?"

"As a clam. Let's go!" Mel said, and started walking toward the rear entrance, his gun gripped tightly at his side.

The building was as quiet as a graveyard. Subdued lighting cast the stairwells and hallways in an eerie glow. The floors and stairs were concrete, absorbing the sound of their footsteps and making it easy to move quietly and without being detected. When Dan and Mel approached the third floor landing, Dan opened the door. They could hear voices. Dan put his finger to his lips, Mel nodded and they both crouched down and went through the door.

The entire third floor was one giant room filled with pallets, crates, old furniture, and boxes. The room was as dimly lit as the rest of the building. The two men duck-walked in the direction of the voices.

"You're just going to let them go?" Manny asked.

"No," Ranker answered. "After we find out where the money is, we'll kill them all."

Dan could see the other door from where he was positioned. There was no sign of Red or Skip. He peeked between two large wooden crates and could see the three men talking. On their rights were Bev, and Steve Durkin, Mel's sister's boyfriend. They were both sitting in wooden chairs with their hands zip-tied behind their backs and rags tied around their mouths. Steve was bloody and bruised, and his left eye was swollen shut.

"And when do we get paid?" Tank Portman asked.

"When I get my money, then you get paid," Ranker bristled. "Don't ask again."

Portman wasn't easily cowered. "Or what?"

"Shut up, Tank," Manny said. "He said he'll pay us, he'll pay us. Calm down."

"How do we know he's not gonna off us too?" Portman demanded.

Dan cursed silently as he heard the door squeak and saw Manny, Portman, and Ranker glance over.

"What was that?" Manny asked.

Ranker looked to Portman. "Go check it out."

Portman folded his tree trunk arms across his boulder chest. "You go check it out."

Ranker put his hand on the holster clipped to his waistband and patted his Glock 23. "Go check it out, asshole."

Portman clenched his teeth and his face reddened, but he did as he was told. Manny and Ranker watched as he crossed the room and exited through the door.

Dan pulled out his weapon.

"How do you know that big moron will just tell you where the money is?" Manny asked.

"Because he's a coward," Ranker said. "He's not the type to fight; he's the type to run … just like he did when we killed his wife and kid."

Dan's eyes shot to Mel, who was pulling back the hammer on his pistol as he stood up. Dan grabbed at Mel's pant leg to stop him but it was too late.

Mel aimed his weapon at Ranker as he moved toward him.

Manny dove behind Bev and Steve, drawing his weapon. When he came to his knees his gun was at Bev's temple.

Ranker's hand moved toward his own gun.

"Don't!" Mel shouted.

Ranker's hand froze.

Dan moved from behind the crates with his weapon drawn.

"Nobody move!" Manny yelled.

Bev stared at Dan, her eyes wide, frantic, pleading.

"Put your guns down on the floor," Manny said.

Dan looked at Mel and then set his gun down. Mel didn't move.

"Drop that gun or I'll waste her." Manny's finger was on the trigger, his hand was shaking.

"You better do as he says, Gormin," Ranker suggested.

Mel stared through the sights and down the barrel at Ranker's fore head.

Ship of Fools

"Don't do it Me—"

Ranker's head exploded like a pound of ground chuck stuffed with a lit M-80.

Manny threw his arm over Bev's shoulder and began firing, using her as a shield.

Dan dove toward his gun.

Bev pushed with her feet as hard as she could, knocking herself and Steve to the floor.

Dan rolled as he grabbed his gun. Coming up onto his knees he fired three shots into Manny's chest.

Mel turned and put one through Manny's cheek, tearing his jaw from his skull. He hit the floor with a whump, landing on his back. His ghastly visage grinned upward, unseeing.

Both men ran to Bev.

Dan ripped the rag from her mouth. "Are you okay?"

"I'm fine."

Mel untied Steve. "You okay, Steve?"

Steve shook his head. Tears were streaming down his face. He was barely conscious. "I didn't tell them anything, Mel, I didn't tell them anything."

Mel took the gag and wiped the blood from Steve's nose. "Where's Stacey, Steve? Where's my sister?" Steve closed his eyes and went limp. Mel felt his neck for a pulse and found one. "He's out."

Red and Skip busted through the door, there guns aimed. Red had two puffy eyes and blood was running from both nostrils. Skip's lip was bleeding, and he had a large red welt on the side of his face.

"Get into some trouble, boys" Dan asked.

"You should see the other dude," Skip answered. "Knocked that Tank right off his treads, didn't we, Red man?"

"You know it, dude," Red replied. They high fived.

"You two quit kissing each other's ass," Dan groused, "and get Steve and Mel to Mel's sister's house, I'll call the cops," He whipped his cell from his pocket.

"Where does she live, dude?" Skip asked.

"Two houses up from the corner," Red answered.

They helped Steve to his feet, and the four men left the room.

Second house from the corner. How did Maxine know that? Dan wondered. *So that's why she didn't want me to go inside her house.* He dialed his phone.

"Hello," Maxine said.

"It's Dan."

"I know."

"It's all over, Maxine. You can bring Stacey back to her house now. It's safe."

There was a short pause. "Okay."

Chapter Forty-Three

Dan sat in his Adirondack chair across from Bev. He had built a small fire, and the two of them were drinking coffee and taking turns with sections of the *Key West Citizen*. Dan stared across the fire at the red marks in the corners of Bev's mouth, a temporary souvenir of the gag.

"How ya feelin'?" Dan asked.

"I'm fine," Bev stated. "My neck is a little sore. How's Mel doing?"

"Richards gave him something to help him sleep. But I expect he'll be up and about any time now. They thought it would be better if I brought him back to the hospital today after everything calmed down, rather than last night while it was all still fresh in his mind."

Bev took a sip of her coffee. "So those bastards killed his wife and daughter. That's so sad."

"Tell me about it. According to his sister, Mel had always thought they had something to do with it, figured it was payback for him stealing the money. She said he

194

blamed himself. She said after they died Mel just lost it, started acting crazier and crazier. She convinced him to pack it up and move as far away as possible."

"I guess this is about as far away as you can get. What did you tell Chief Carver?"

"We told him the truth about everything except for the part about Mel stealing the money, and Mel and Stacey actually having the money."

"So they'll get to keep it?"

"Why not? They pay out of pocket for Mel's stay at the hospital. Without that money, they couldn't afford it."

"And Stacey was staying at Maxine's the whole time."

"Yup. Maxine said Stacey came to her a couple weeks ago and told her she needed someplace to hide. She said she had seen Lasko and Ranker coming out of a bar on Duval Street. She knew they were looking for Mel."

The back door swung open, and Mel walked out showered, dressed, and ready to go. He had a cup of coffee in his hand. "Thought I'd try a cup of coffee today," he commented as he walked up to the fire. Dan and Bev noticed that he was unusually calm.

Dan got up from his chair. "Here, sit down. I'll grab a lawn chair."

"No, that's okay," Mel replied. "We better get going, no sense in postponing the inevitable." He turned to Bev and held out his hand. "It was very nice to meet you, beautiful Bev. I'm sorry our date was cut short."

Bev took his hand; she stood and gave him a hug. "Me too, Mel."

Mel turned and lumbered up the gravel path that led to the driveway.

Dan walked over to his shed, went inside, and walked back out with a pair of bolt cutters. "I guess we're out of here," he said.

"What do you need those for?" Bev asked.

"You never know when you might need a good pair of bolt cutters, Bev."

"Oh, one other thing. Where did Stacey have the money hidden?"

Dan turned and started across the yard. "Didn't ask."

*****

Dan took a left onto Catherine Street, pulled the Bug to the side of the street and parked.

"What are we doing back here?" Mel asked.

"Come on," Dan replied, grabbing his bolt cutters. "Let's go for a drive."

The two men climbed from the car and walked up to the gate. Dan cut the chain and slid the gate open.

"We could get in trouble for this," Mel said.

Dan yanked the tarp off of the Ferrari. "Nah, if anybody hassles us, just flash them your badge. Your real one, that is."

Mel smiled and opened the door. The key lay in the driver's seat next to the small magnetic box where he had dropped it the night before.

Dan walked around the car and got in the passenger side.

Mel turned the key and the engine roared. "I love that sound," he said.

"Better put the top down."

Mel pulled up to the gate and looked both ways. "Dan, I just remembered: I don't have a driver's license!"

Dan shrugged. "So what."

"Yeah. So what."

Dan reached over and turned on the radio, "One Particular Harbour" blasted from the speakers.

"Which way should I go?" Mel asked.

That's up to you, pal."

The End

COMING JUNE 2015

Jake Stellar
Beach Shoot

COMING AUGUST 2015

Return to Dunquin Cove

ALSO BY RODNEY RIESEL

Sleeping Dogs Lie
From the Tales of Dan Coast

A mystery set in the Florida Keys follows Dan Coast, an unlicensed private detective of sorts, as he is hired to find the missing boyfriend of a woman who herself soon ends up missing. When someone from the woman's past unexpectedly shows up at Dan's home, with a story of faked deaths and missing life insurance money; Dan along with his sidekick Red set out to find the money, and the woman.

ISBN: 978-0-9883503-0-4

Ocean Floors
From the Tales of Dan Coast

The second installment in the Dan Coast series, Ocean Floors, is a tale of mystery and possible romance when a chance meeting with a beautiful young woman leads Dan and his trusted sidekick Red down a road of murder and kidnapping. Join Dan and Red as they try to solve the murder while searching for a missing friend.

ISBN: 978-0-9894877-0-2

Impaled

An Adirondack Short Story

Eric Stone is an investigator with The Town of Webb Police Department. Chuck Little is Head Ranger at the Nick's Lake campground. An unlikely duo, together they work to solve a murder that mimics a spree of gruesome murders taking place years earlier. Is it a copycat, or has the murderer resurfaced after all of these years? Join Stone and Little as they piece together the clues to solve this mystery taking place in the small village of Old Forge in the Adirondack Mountains.

North Murder Beach

A Jake Stellar Novel

The first installment of the story of North Myrtle Beach police detective, Jake Stellar. The spring bike rallies have ended, the spring breakers have all gone back to school, and the summer tourist season is a few weeks away. What better time for a police officer to take a nice quiet relaxing week off from work? That's what Jake Stellar had in mind. That is until someone from his past resurfaces to remind him of a terrible secret he has spent years trying to forget. In North Murder Beach, a story of revenge, Jake is unwillingly and violently forced to confront his secret from his past.

ISBN: 978-0-9894877-1-9

The Coast of Christmas Past
From the Tales of Dan Coast

Coast of Christmas Past is the third book in the Dan Coast series of books. Dan Coast is all set to spend Christmas just the same way he has every year for the past few years; alone and drunk. But when uninvited, unexpected guests arrive and throw a wrench into his holiday plans he is forced to sober up (slightly), and throw on a smile. Just when it seems nothing else could go wrong, a close friend is injured in what appears, to the police, to be a drug deal gone bad. Dan Coast and his sidekick, Red jump into action to find the truth while their friend lies unconscious in the hospital.

ISBN: 978-0-9894877-3-3

The Man in Room Number Four

When a mysterious stranger arrives in the small coastal town of Dunquin Cove, Maine it appears as though Claire and her young son, Mica's prayers have been answer. But who is he, and why is he really here? Join Claire and her guests at the Colsome House Bed and Breakfast as they piece together the mystery of the Man in Room Number Four.

ISBN: 978-0-9894877-2-6